Summer's End

A Halloween Novella

By

Lisa Morton

JournalStone
San Francisco

This is a work of fiction. All of the characters, names, incidents, organizations, and dialogue in this novel are either the products of the author's imagination or are used fictitiously.

JournalStone books may be ordered through booksellers or by contacting:

JournalStone
www.journalstone.com

www.journal-store.com

ISBN: 978-1-940161-03-7 *(sc)*
ISBN: 978-1-940161-18-1 *(hc)*
ISBN: 978-1-940161-04-4 *(ebook)*

Library of Congress Control Number: 2013941617

Printed in the United States of America
JournalStone rev. date: October 4, 2013

Cover Design: *Denise Daniel*
Cover Art: *Harry Morris*
Edited by: *Norman Rubenstein*

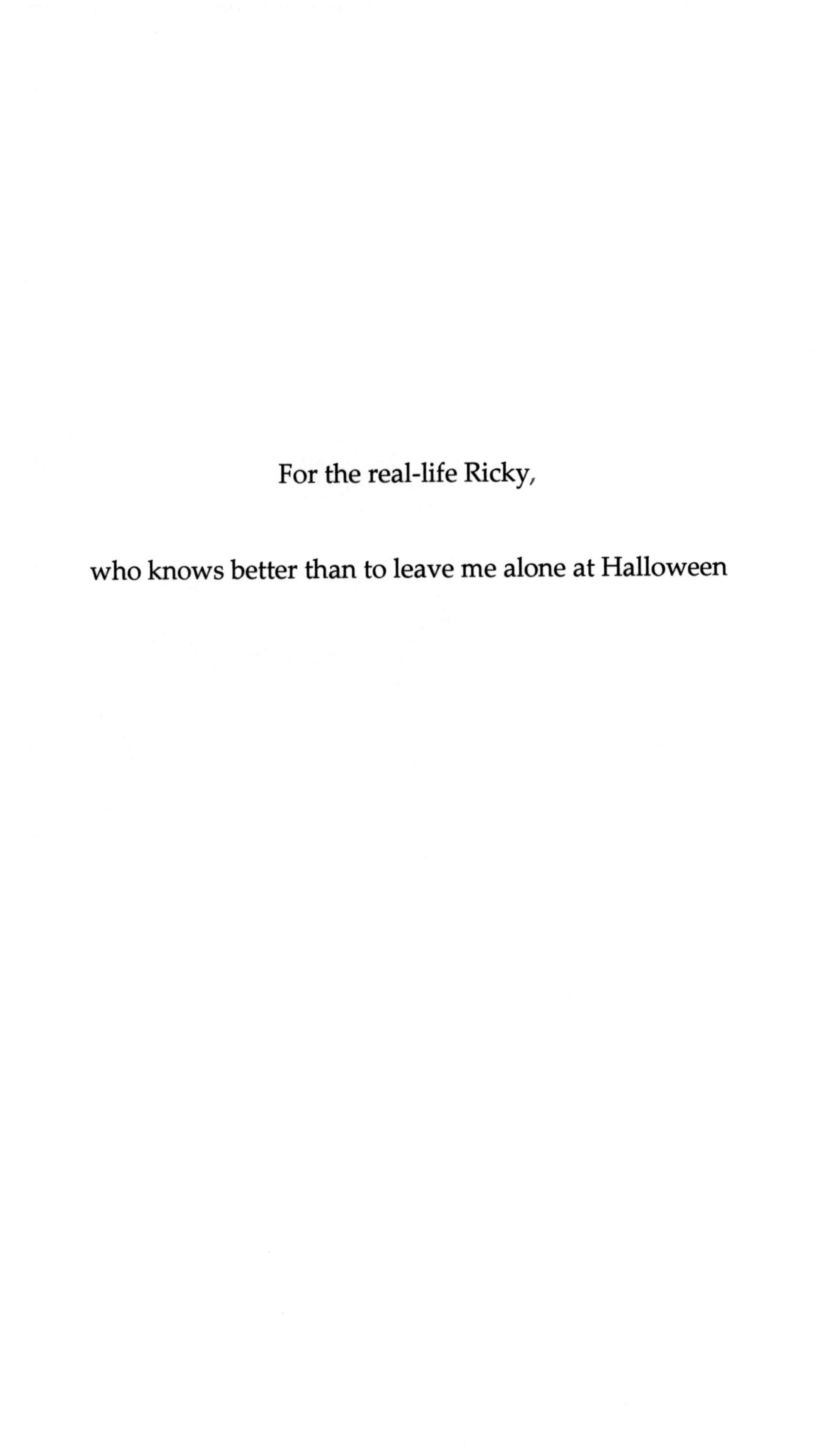

For the real-life Ricky,

who knows better than to leave me alone at Halloween

Endorsements

"With her new novella, *Summer's End,* Lisa Morton achieves something rare, arguably unique: she creates a genre that can be defined only by this piece of work. This challenging, exhilarating, darkly-humored, heartbreaking work is hands-down brilliant, the best work she's ever done; it's been a long time since the boundaries between the book and its author have been so expertly blurred, trapping the reader in the oppressive , nerve-wracking gray area between. Don't start reading with any preconceived notions about horror *or* storytelling because they'll be shredded into confetti and scattered to the dark winds. Just steel yourself for a reading experience that will rival any other piece of work you will encounter this year." – **Gary A. Braunbeck** Bram Stoker Award-winning author of *To Each Their Darkness*

"In *Summer's End,* Lisa Morton has created something so strikingly unique that it stands alone in the genre. All writers pull their work from inside themselves, but Morton has literally put herself inside the work, and she has pulled it off so beautifully, so seamlessly, that it does not read like fiction — it reads like an account of actual events. Her extensive knowledge of her subject and her impeccable skills as a writer and storyteller are combined in a wicked and delightful potion that gave me *real* goosebumps, *real* chills, and reminded me that horror fiction can and *should* frighten the hell out of the reader. *Summer's End* is a thin volume, but it is a formidable achievement. I'll never look at a jack-o'-lantern the same way again." – **Ray Garton** Author of *Live Girls* and *Meds.*

"Samhain, says Lhwyd, is compounded of Samb, summer and fhuin the end: this is a false derivation...the Druids taught that Samhain at this season called the souls to judgment; hence Samhain was named BALSAB, or Dominus mortis, for Bal is Lord, and Sab death."

Charles Vallancey, "Of Allhallow Eve" from *Collectanea de rebus Hibernicis Volume 3* (1786)

"General Vallancey, though a man of learning, wrote more nonsense than any man of his time."

London Quarterly Review, April 1818

October 31, 2012

Almost Midnight

My name is Lisa Morton. I'm one of the world's leading authorities on Halloween.

And this year I discovered that everything I thought I knew, was wrong.

October 20, 2012

It's been less than two weeks since the world started to fall apart.

During the third week of October, I received an e-mail with the subject line "Samhain query." Of course, I get a lot of e-mailed questions this time of year: Requests for interviews, reporters searching for illustrations for Halloween articles, someone trying to identify and appraise an odd Halloween collectible. This year I had a new Halloween history book out, so I was trying to set up book signings. I'd even been invited to sign at a store in Salem, home of America's own homegrown witch-hunting tragedy, although they couldn't find me a place to stay; hotels there book up a year in advance for the October festivities.

But, two things stood out about this e-mail: The first was that it asked not about Halloween, but about the holiday's ancient Celtic forebear. The second was that the sender's address ended in "ucla.edu."

I clicked on the message and read:

Dear Ms. Morton –

I'm a linguistics professor at UCLA specializing in Latin, and I'm currently working with a team from Ireland to translate a manuscript discovered in a recent archaeological dig. The manuscript was written mostly in Latin, but was believed to belong to an Irish Druid circa 350 C.E. It includes numerous references to Samhain, many of which I'm frankly having difficulty making sense of. I found your book *The Halloween Encyclopedia* in the campus library, and you seem to have extensive knowledge of Samhain. Your bio says you're in the Southern California area, so would you be open to a meeting? Thank you. My contact information is below.

Sincerely,
Dr. Wilson Armitage[1]

I checked the e-mail headers to make sure this really had come from UCLA, because otherwise I would have smiled and dismissed it as an early Halloween prank. The Celts' Druids—essentially their priest caste—were notorious for passing all of their lore verbally; they didn't believe in writing anything down. To have a Druid "manuscript," then, was virtually impossible. And in Latin? There had been cases of Celts who had integrated into Roman society and become quite adept in Latin, but they were from the Gaul tribes of continental Europe, not Ireland.

But, if this was real…

Scholars frankly know little about the Irish Celts, and less about Samhain. What we have are the tantalizing bits passed down in legends transcribed by early Catholic missionaries. Stories about heroes who fought malicious *sidh,* or fairies, on Samhain Eve[2]. Horror tales involving hanged corpses that returned to vengeful life on that night and asked for drinks, which they spit into the faces of those who were foolish enough to supply them, causing immediate death to their benefactors[3]. Romances about princesses who turned into swans on October 31st and who flew off with their true love[4]. There were suggestions that the Celts had celebrated "summer's end" (the literal translation of "Samhain") with a three-day long party of drinking, feasting and horse racing. One debate raging among those who

---

[1] Dr. Wilson Armitage is the author of *Latin: A Comprehensive Study of the Language*, now in its ninth edition.
[2] "The Coming of Finn"
[3] "The Story of Nera"
[4] "The Story of Oengus"

study Halloween questions how much our modern holiday owes to the Celts. Some believe that the festival has a completely Christian history, and that its grimmer aspects derive from the November 2nd Catholic celebration of All Souls. Myself, I fall largely on the side of "summer's end"—I think Halloween unquestionably inherited some of its lore from Samhain, like belief in supernatural forces being prevalent on the evening of October 31st, or the notion (held mainly by the old Scots) that fortune-telling was likelier to be successful if performed on All Hallows Eve.

There's another camp, however, which holds that Halloween is little more than a pagan festival renamed; fundamentalist Christians go so far as to condemn the holiday as a celebration of "Samhain, Lord of the Dead."[5] What the fire-and-brimstone preachers don't know is that their "facts" stem from the fanciful work of one Charles Vallancey, an eighteenth-century British engineer who was dispatched by the government to survey Ireland. He fell in love with the Irish/Celtic language and culture, and spent most of the rest of his life collecting information, which he transcribed into a massive opus (pretentiously) called Collectanea de rebus Hibernicis. Except...Vallancey was frankly an arrogant fool. He was obsessed with the notion that the Celtic tongue could be traced back to Indo-European roots, and in his quest to find connections he frequently disposed of the facts. He somehow decided that all of the other scholars (and there had already been many even by 1786, when his Collectanea was published) were wrong, and that Samhain had not been a new year's celebration and in-bringing of the harvest, but was rather a day of judgment when the Celts offered sacrifices to their dark god "Bal-Sab." Vallancey's books found their way onto library shelves around the world, next to volumes that both reiterated and decried them, and so Vallancey inadvertently created a strange alternate history of Halloween. By the 1990s, some American church groups were calling October 31st "The Devil's Birthday" and they consequently banned trick or treat. I

[5] http://www.churchesofchrist.net/authors/Walter_Porter/Halloween.htm

wondered if they were simply miserable people who didn't want their kids to have any fun, either.

So now I had been presented with what could potentially, possibly, change our understanding of Samhain and perhaps finally lay the ghost of Vallancey to rest. My schedule was pretty booked, but I had a rare free night tomorrow, and my significant other, Ricky, was working on a movie that was shooting down in South Carolina (he's an actor, and is most well known for his performance as "Henry the Red" in Army of Darkness). I answered Dr. Armitage and told him I'd be happy to meet tomorrow to discuss his project. He responded within minutes, suggesting a time and providing his UCLA office address.

At least Armitage was legit, and he wasn't likely to be the kind of man who could be fooled by a scam. What would I find out? Was Samhain mainly an administrative function when the Celts extinguished all their home hearths and relit them with an ember from a fire kindled by Druid priests (for which services they were duly taxed)? Was it really a three-day kegger? Was it possible that human sacrifice had been performed?

I was twenty-four hours away from finding out.

October 21, 2012

Evening

Wilson Armitage turned out to be one of those college professors who you knew had girls fighting to sign up for his classes—he was maybe 35, with a charmingly ragged haircut, a quick smile, and clothes straight from Urban Outfitters. His office was more old-fashioned than he was, full of language reference books and stacks of papers and jars of pencils; only one small laptop on the desk offering evidence of the 21st century.

If I liked Wilson immediately, I was less sure about the man with him: Thin, fifty-something, with narrow features and a perpetual scowl. Wilson introduced him as Dr. Conor ó Cuinn, the archaeologist who had overseen the excavation at which the manuscript had been found. He'd flown over from Ireland with the actual artifact, which UCLA was still in the process of scanning. Wilson did most of the talking, but Conor never stopped staring at me. It occurred to me to wonder if he simply mistrusted women. Or perhaps American women?

Wilson started by offering me a chair, then turned his laptop around to let me look at pages of the manuscript while he talked. The photos on the screen showed a continuous scroll, broken into frames for scanning, with edges chewed and uneven; the parchment or vellum was covered in neat handwriting that I just barely recognized as Latin. The scroll had been wrapped in oiled cloth and laid within a metal box with sealed edges—a box still clutched by the bony fingers of a long-dead female corpse. A poor farmer in Northern Ireland had discovered the remains while digging peat blocks out of a bog. Fortunately he'd had enough sense to call the authorities, who'd brought in ó Cuinn. The excavation had been brief—there'd been nothing else at all in the bog—but the scroll was remarkable. The author had been named Mongfind[6], and claimed to have been the last of the Irish Druids.

"Well, right off the bat, something's odd," I said, "that's a female name, and most of the Druids were men, although there are isolated historical recordings of female Druids."

The two professors exchanged a quick glance, and then Wilson smiled. "You're going to be in for a few surprises, I think. According to this...exactly half the Druid caste were women, and they were essential to the Druid rituals."

I couldn't even answer, not right away. Half the Druids were women? "How do you know this isn't a fraud?"

Wilson shot a glance at his Irish companion, who nodded back to him. "We've got everything from carbon dating to Mongfind's body to confirm this."

"So you think the body you found this with was Mongfind herself?"

"We believe so—Mongfind mentions several...uh, peculiarities of her body that matched up to the corpse found in the bog. We've even got autopsy results on the body confirming how she died, how old she was, and what she ate for her last meal. And of course, Dr. ó Cuinn is a highly regarded specialist in his field. No, the evidence is incontrovertible."

ó Cuinn spoke up, and his brogue was thick and obvious, even with only two words spoken. "The tongue..."

Armitage made a quick grimace, then added, "Of course. One of those 'peculiarities' mentioned in the manuscript is that Mongfind's tongue was cut out. The body we found had been mutilated in that manner."

"Why was her tongue cut out?"

Armitage took a deep breath and then said, "What do you know about the conversion of the Celts to Christianity?"

---

[6] Mongfind is a legendary sorceress and warrior queen who supposedly died one Samhain when she ingested poison meant for her brother.

I shrugged. "As much as anyone, I guess. Gregory the Great taught his missionaries the doctrine of syncretism[7], of incorporating existing pagan practices rather than stamping them out. All Saints' Day was probably moved from May 13th to November 1st to help Catholic missionaries in Ireland convert the Celts[8]."

ó Cuinn asked, "Have you not wondered why the Celts would have so easily converted?"

In fact, I had. I figured that more often than not, conversion had been along the lines of the conquest of the Aztecs, when Cortez had ridden into their lands with a banner that read "We shall conquer under the sign of the cross" and a large force of men with superior armor, weapons, and diseases that the Aztecs couldn't fight. "Sure, I've wondered that, but I figured they probably kind of bought them off with a combination of gifts and threats."

"According to this..." Armitage gestured at the laptop screen, "...the Catholic missionaries had studied the tactics employed by Roman troops against the British Celts, and they learned. When they were ready, they moved into Ireland with a hired army and started by slaughtering all of the Celt warriors, then moved onto the Druids. Only a few escaped; the remaining Celts converted easily."

"So you're telling me this document reveals that early Catholic missionaries were basically mass murderers?"

"Well, more in the nature of...conquerors," Wilson said, squirming, then riffling through a stack of printouts on his desk. "Listen to this: 'Yesterday the Catholics offered a gift of a great man built of wicker. This figure could hold fifty men, and the Catholics suggested we should tour it from the inside. When fifty of us were within, they sealed the entrance and set the wicker man afire. The rest of us tried to save our fellows, but our enemies had sunk traps in the earth, and many of our tribe died impaled on great spikes. Those

---

[7] In a famous letter from 601 A.D., Pope Gregory (later known as Gregory the Great) instructed the Abbot Mellitus, who was then bound for Britain, to leave pagan temples standing, because "if those temples are well built, it is requisite that they be converted from the worship of devils to the service of the true God."

[8] May 13th had probably been chosen as the original date for All Saints Day because it had marked the climax of Lemuria, a Roman festival honoring the dead.

of us who suffered neither stakes nor flames were forced to listen to the dying screams of our brothers and sisters.'"

I couldn't suppress a laugh. "This is all going to go over well with modern Catholics."

But bitter jokes aside, my head was spinning. Hadn't it been Caesar who had ascribed wicker men to the Celts[9]? Yet now we had something saying the infamous giant figures were not Celtic, but had been used as a trick by Catholic missionaries...who were also ruthless invaders. "So...are you suggesting that all of the other histories..."

ó Cuinn leaned forward, his pinched features eager. "...are false, re-written by later Christian scribes who were instructed to hide the truth."

"Why?" Even as I asked it, I knew the answer.

Wilson confirmed. "Don't the victors in every war write the history they want? The Catholics probably weren't comfortable with a society in which women held half the religious offices and..."

"And what?"

Wilson abruptly dropped his eyes and fidgeted; he was uneasy talking about whatever came next. I looked to ó Cuinn, who slid a USB stick across the table to me. "It might be easier if you just read what Dr. Armitage has translated thus far."

I picked the stick up. "I can take this?"

They both nodded, so I put it in a pocket. "Okay. But...you called me in with questions about Samhain, and you haven't even mentioned that."

Nodding toward the stick, Wilson said, "Read that and you'll see. According to our Druid priestess Mongfind, Samhain was a little more than a new year's party. It was..." He trailed off, unsure, or simply unwilling to tell me.

"What?"

ó Cuinn filled in. "According to this...the Druids could perform real magic, and on Samhain they communed directly with their gods."

I'm sure my mouth was open as I stared at ó Cuinn; I expected him to wink, or laugh.

He didn't.

---

[9] *The Conquest of Gaul*

October 21
-
October 22

> I am Mongfind, daughter of Fidach of Munster, and a devoted sister of the Morrigan. I was once the Arch-Druid of Ireland, but now I am simply the last Druid. Last night was Samhain, and I attempted to speak to the gods. I failed. When I have finished writing this, the Druids will be no more.

That was how the manuscript began.

I stayed up all night reading it. Wilson had translated around 30,000 words so far—he was still working through the rest—but I understood now why they'd made me sign a nondisclosure agreement before I'd left the office.

This would change everything. Not just our knowledge of the Celts, but of the Romans, the Christians, and much of what came after.

Mongfind began by talking about her childhood, focusing on how she'd begun training in the Druid priesthood from the age of six. She memorized thousands of pieces of history, religious ritual, law, and herbal knowledge. By the age of 16, she could recite thousands of lengthy chants, or prepare potions that would cure any disease. She described a world of golden palaces and well-fed, happy citizens, of bards who performed magnificent poems and noble warriors who fought off enemies with ease. According to her, the Celts had skilled astronomers who had already charted the solar system, seamen who regularly visited America, and farmers who could produce grains and vegetables that remained fresh through the dead of winter.

She also claimed that the Celts owed their good fortune to their gods, who were quite real and visited each Samhain.

The original manuscript had been a mishmash of Mongfind's own life, the history of the Irish Celts, and Druidic rituals. As the manuscript progressed, the sections on her own life had become less detailed, more rushed, and I soon found out why.

The missionaries had timed their armies to arrive shortly before Samhain, when they knew the warriors would be settling into their winter quarters and the rest of the country preparing for the festivities. The Samhain rituals in essence renewed the Celts' contracts with their gods, and the gods' communion with their mortal worshippers was at a low point just before. The invaders' strategies had been thought out for decades, and were carried out with ruthless efficiency; they laid waste to the Celts' nobility and warriors, silenced and imprisoned the Druids, and enslaved the rest. The Catholics had inadvertently killed many of the Druids when they'd cut their tongues out to ensure that they would be unable to call for their gods. Mongfind had been mutilated with all the rest, but had found one piece of luck the others hadn't: A sympathetic Catholic missionary. From her journal:

> One day I arrived at the place where I thought I would spend the remainder of my life: One of our great halls, now a home for our conquerors. My cell here was better—I was provided with straw to sleep on, and there was a high window large enough to permit nearly an hour of sunlight to penetrate each afternoon.
>
> The man in charge of this place visited me as soon as I arrived. We were of course unable to communicate—even if we knew each others' languages, I had no tongue to convey words with—but he gave me to understand that he intended me no harm. The others treated him with reverence, and I realized he was in charge of this place. He

pointed at himself and said the word, "Jerome,"[10] which I took to be his name.

He made sure I received generous amounts of food and blankets, and I soon began to recover some of the health I had lost after my initial capture. As he visited me each day, he brought long rolls of paper, ink, and quill, and taught me words from his language, which he called Latin. I was at first unwilling to use the quill, but reconciled myself soon enough—how could it be against the gods to learn of his world and language?

I quickly became quite adept at writing in Latin, and Jerome—whose title was "Abbot", while his house was called "monastery"—was very pleased. He began to urge me to write of my people and our history. At first I refused, and he accepted my explanation that we didn't believe in committing to mere paper that which we held sacred.

But one day Jerome arrived at my cell very early in the morning; it was not yet sunrise, and he woke me. He said he'd just received word that the Church had issued orders for the remaining Druids to be put to death.

Then he took me from the cell, led me out of the monastery, and brought me to where he had a horse waiting. He told me that this was the only time he'd disobeyed his Church, and that he would spend the rest of his days begging his God to forgive him. He'd provided my mount with supplies, including food, clothing, tools...and ink and paper. I

---

[10] Abbot Jerome is apparently lost to history. Strangely enough, the timing—mid-4th-century—coincides with the life of St. Jerome, an early church father who was involved with translations of the Old Testament from the Hebrew; however, it seems extremely unlikely that St. Jerome ever journeyed as far north as Great Britain and Ireland, so this is evidently another Jerome. It's also worth noting that Mongfind's journal contains no mention of Ireland's patron saint, Patrick...but then it would be unlikely to find Patrick in her journal, since he historically appears in Ireland almost a century later. Perhaps Patrick was always intended to be sent in as a sort of compassionate, unifying figure after the horrors of the earlier missionaries.

thanked him profusely, communicated to him he would have made a fine Druid, and left him forever.

I knew not this part of Eire, but a day's ride brought me to uninhabited woodland, with plentiful game and water. I was well trained in Celtic survival arts, and knew I could make a home here. Whether I could avoid the Romans forever...well, only the Dagda and the Morrigan[11] knew that for certain.

It was a hard life, and lonely, and I did not fare well as the year grew colder. I was able to call upon the *sidh* for some assistance, and when I needed to hunt I allowed the Morrigan to fill me...but without a Druid of the opposite sex, I was unable to call down the Dagda or even bring the Morrigan's full powers into play. Samhain came and went, and I could offer only a small sacrifice—a fox I'd captured and held for that night. It was not enough.

Within a month I knew I was dying.

Although Jerome's consideration had led me to believe I was healed, the mutilation of my mouth by his fellows began to plague me, and with the onset of winter cold I fell ill. I knew I could hold on for a short time, but doubted I would live to see Beltane[12].

Beyond my own death, however, loomed a greater horror: If I was the last remaining Druid, all of our knowledge would die with me.

Unless I committed the greatest of sins and recorded it all.

I could, with the language and utensils Jerome had provided. I knew I wouldn't have time to write all I knew, but if I began now, I might have just enough left for the most important things, the rituals

---

[11] In Celtic religion, the Dagda and the Morrigan are basically the father and mother gods (respectively). They were thought to couple at Samhain to ensure fertility for the next year's crops and livestock, and they figure prominently in a number of existing Samhain legends (the Morrigan, for example, was also a warrior who, together with her son Oengus, drove the monstrous Fomorians from Ireland one Samhain).

[12] In the Celtic calendar, Beltane— which takes place on May Eve, exactly six months apart from Samhain, or Halloween—was the great spring/summer counterpart to the fall/winter holiday.

and stories and formulae that every Druid learned in their first year.

And so I begged the gods' forgiveness and I wrote.

It was more difficult than I'd expected, especially as winter set in. I built small fires for no other reason than to thaw my ink and my cramped fingers. I resented time taken away from the task of writing—time to hunt, to prepare food, to attend to other bodily needs. I realized my thoughts were not organized, that recollections of my own life (which I selfishly thought important enough to commit here) were bound with the true knowledge.

Yet it kept me alive. Even as I grew weaker and thinner, even as the spittle I coughed up began to contain more blood than other fluid, I kept writing. I burned with the need to record, and my own heat carried me through to Beltane and beyond.

But as another Samhain approached, my fingers finally refused to work, and my eyes grew dim. It was enough; I'd written only a fraction of our learning, but it would do. What was here could provide a new beginning, should it be found by one of understanding.

As my body failed me, I settled on one last plan:

I would journey to a nearby bog, and on Samhain I would offer myself as sacrifice there, asking the thick waters to preserve me and hide me until one would come who was worthy of receiving this, the last of our real soul. I will wrap these pages carefully in animal hides and a box Jerome provided, and take them beneath the water with me, trusting in the gods to keep us both.

Forgive me, holy ones. I know I've failed you twice now and damned the world to a new darkness, but perhaps one day our light will shine again, if my sacrifice is accepted.

I dream of a new world.

There were still pages after that—apparently Mongfind had remembered a last few items to commit to history. But her story really ended there. In the bog where she and her pages were found, more than fifteen hundred years later.

And she'd been right about at least one thing: The world had descended into "a new darkness." The Dark Ages settled over Europe and continued for a thousand years, ten bleak centuries of ignorance and confusion that climaxed as the Black Death raced across the continent while the Church burned tens of thousands of so-called witches and tortured heretics.

Despite the Enlightenment and the Renaissance and the Industrial Revolution and the Digital Age, I couldn't help but wonder if the world had ever really recovered. Especially recently, as I passed each year more convinced that mankind was entering its own final chapter, that centuries of greed and ecological devastation were finally leading to a planet that would no longer be able to sustain so many of us.

I was less certain what to make of Mongfind's accounts of encounters with *sidh,* of using magic to ward off foes (before the missionaries had slain the Druids), and especially of blood sacrifices on Samhain to propitiate the gods. The knowledge Mongfind had recorded was a mix of what seemed to be practical information—which healing herbs could be gathered in a forest, when to plant certain crops, how to create "needfire," or sparks engendered by friction—but other parts of the recorded lore read like a fantasy novel. There was an account of a Samhain when the *sidh* had appeared in the king's throne room, demanding tribute of food and slaves, but Mongfind and a male arch-Druid name Mog Roith had sacrificed a black sheep and a young warrior who'd offered himself to invoke a fearsome and powerful death-spirit named Bal-sab, who had driven the *sidh* back to the barrow they'd emerged from. Mog Roith and Mongfind had spent the next two weeks not sleeping or eating, but working first to banish Bal-sab, and then to create a spell that would seal the barrow forever.

Bal-sab...Charles Vallancey's "lord of death." There was more about Bal-sab and Samhain: Apparently each Samhain, sacrifices were offered to Bal-sab to ensure his cooperation throughout the coming year. If they bought him off with a few small deaths at the end of every summer, he apparently spared the Celts from plagues and wars and pestilence the rest of the year.

Dear God. Vallancey's ludicrous ramblings suddenly didn't seem so ludicrous anymore. Instead, he'd been right all along. We were the fools, not Vallancey. The alternate history of Halloween was the real history.

All of this was presented in Wilson's straightforward, matter-of-fact translation, which made it all sound perfectly plausible. I really didn't know what to think of it.

I was going over it again when my phone rang. Checking the caller ID, I saw "Ó CUINN, CONOR." I'd given Wilson my number, but somehow I wasn't entirely comfortable knowing that ó Cuinn had it.

The conversation that followed didn't do much to dissuade me in finding Dr. ó Cuinn unnerving. He wanted to meet. His Irish accent was anything but lilting; he sounded excited and anxious. I asked what he wanted to meet about.

"Have you read the journal?"

"Yes. Or at least most it."

"What do you make of it?"

"I'm not sure."

"Well, maybe I can help. I've got some ideas on it, but...well, we should discuss it in person."

I debated for a few seconds. I could tell him I was busy (which was true; in fact, I had two book signings and four interviews scheduled over the next week). I could ask that he just e-mail me whatever he had to say. But then I reminded myself that this man was a respected archaeologist, an expert in a field I'd once seriously considered pursuing. He undoubtedly did have some insight into the find, and I was curious to know why he wanted to share his thoughts with me.

"All right," I told him. "Did you have somewhere in mind?"

He had his own temporary office at the UCLA campus. He wanted to meet tonight.

I almost said no. I'd attended UCLA as an undergraduate, and the place hadn't changed much since then. It was spread out and dark, with parking structures nowhere near any of the buildings. This was a Monday night in fall, so the campus would be quiet: No sporting events or film screenings at Melnitz Hall, no crowds of students to feel safe within. When I'd attended the school, I'd lived in one of the dorms to the west of the grounds; they'd routinely issued warnings to female students about the dangers of walking alone after dark. I'd even written a recent short story in which a male student had been attacked here by a transgendered rapist.[13]

But I was intrigued—did he know something about Samhain? I'd googled Conor ó Cuinn, and his credentials were solid; not overwhelming, but he'd overseen enough excavations around Ireland that he was considered something of an expert in Celtic history.

That brought up a new question in my mind: Why had they called me in? There was surely nothing I could offer above what was in my books. There had to be some other reason they hadn't revealed yet. Maybe they were just doing a documentary for The History Channel and needed another talking head.

So I said yes, and by 8 p.m. I was parked and making my way across the campus grounds. It was a mid-October night in L.A., which meant it was still warm enough to need only a light jacket. The campus was mostly empty; in fact, it seemed too empty. Surely classes were in session in October, and a state university must have certainly offered *some* evening classes? I saw only a handful of students, all hunched over and hurrying somewhere as if anxious to escape a chill that didn't even exist.

I was just passing a thick growth of shrubbery ringing the edge of one of the great brick-built halls when I first heard it: A slight rustling of the leaves. The night was still, there was no breeze to blame, and I swallowed down a small jolt of unease. I scanned the low bushes, trying not to appear too obvious, but saw no movement, nor heard anything else. A squirrel, then, or maybe a cat strayed over from the surrounding residential area…

---

[13] "Dr. Jekyll and Mr. Hyde" from *Monsters of L.A.*

Something struck the brickwork ahead and to the right of me. The tiny, metallic clang was followed by what sounded for all the world like a stifled laugh.

This time I did stop, peering into the dark corner from which the sounds had emanated. I wished then that I carried a flashlight, one of those little mags that dangles on a keychain; or even a lighter. As it was, I could make out nothing in the black shadow surrounding the looming three-story building.

I waited for a few seconds, ears straining, but heard nothing else. The echo of a distant cell phone conversation, yes; or something coming from within the building, possibly traveling through a ventilation duct. That was it.

I continued on; the hall where ó Cuinn had said his temporary office was housed couldn't be more than a hundred yards off now. I was sure it was the next building ahead, and I'd be safe once I was inside—

Something scuttled through the bushes just a few feet to my left now, and all speculation was done. I reached into the jacket pocket where I'd put my car keys, and wrapped a fist around them; if I had to fight off an attacker, they might think twice after getting a key wrapped between two knuckles in the face. But I still started walking fast, toward the building, trying not to look over my shoulder, trying to ignore the obvious sound of something now following me, something getting closer with each step. Suddenly I was shivering, and my breath puffed out in front of me—how was that possible?—and I almost ran the last bit to the double doors leading into the hall, to the warmth and safety of the well-lit interior beyond…

What if the doors are locked? That thought flickered through my growing unease as I leapt up the five steps to the landing, reached out for the door, tried not to imagine being caught there, in front of the doors, alone, by whatever tracked me…

I flung the door open and stepped through.

As the door closed behind me, I turned and looked out.

There was nothing there.

I actually walked right up to the glass, scanning the night. I'm not someone who frightens easily; maybe it's because I explore fear so often in fiction. I have no phobias, and being a lifelong city dweller (and occasionally working as a screenwriter in the film industry, where the writer is everyone's doormat), I'd developed a tough hide. I'd been followed before...but I'd never been followed like this.

"Ms. Morton?"

I spun so fast I nearly tripped on my own feet. Conor ó Cuinn stood behind me; I'd been so intent on looking outside that I hadn't heard him approach. I have to say that as much as he put me on edge, he was still preferable to whatever had just followed me.

"Are you all right?"

"Yes, I...sorry, I think someone just followed me here."

ó Cuinn's reaction to that was unexpected, to say the least—he glanced quickly past me, and then smiled. "Yes, well...perhaps we can talk in my office."

It was such an inappropriate response that I wanted to shout at him; I would've turned around and left, except that something was still out there. Something that didn't seem to shock Dr. Conor ó Cuinn.

It crossed my mind then to wonder if what had followed me had been ó Cuinn himself. Could he have somehow beat me to the entrance, or used some other way into the building? Or even put someone else up to it? But why?

"Dr. ó Cuinn..."

"Call me Conor." He gestured down the hallway. "Please."

I followed him. At least that way he was ahead of me, always in sight.

ó Cuinn's "office" turned out to be little more than a storage closet, with boxes lining two walls, a window with the blinds drawn over it on a third wall, and beat-up metal desk and threadbare chair against the fourth. On the desk were a tablet computer and plug-in keyboard, a pen, a pad of paper, and a few books. He gestured at a metal folding chair pushed up against the cardboard crates, and he took the ancient rolling chair behind the desk.

"I'm sorry, I don't have anything to offer you..." He waved a hand around the space, indicating the lack of coffee maker or even water cooler.

"That's okay, but I..." I decided to be honest with him and see how he reacted. "Something was definitely after me just now, outside."

He peered at me for an instant, and I found myself disliking his narrow features and dark eyes (black Irish) all over again. After a few seconds, he looked away and asked, "So, you said you've read most of the manuscript?"

"Most of it, yes. I haven't looked at some of the longer sections in detail yet, the..."

"Spells?"

"Well...yes." There were lengthy sections of the manuscript that seemed to be little more than very precise descriptions of rituals and ceremonies, or how to gather and dry certain herbs, or how to enact what could only be called "spells." I'd glanced at a few of them, but had tuned out when I'd seen words like "wand" and "sacrifice."

I should probably mention here that I'm a confirmed, die-hard skeptic, and always have been. I've never believed in ghosts, UFOs, Bigfoot, Nessie, reincarnation, conspiracy theories (most of them, anyway), demonic possession (although I'd like to—it would explain a lot), Echinacea's ability to prevent a cold, Mount Olympus, trickle-down economics, chupacabras, magic (other than illusion), vampires, werewolves, or any religion you'd care to offer up. I'm a longtime subscriber to Skeptical Inquirer magazine, and for entertainment I enjoy watching YouTube videos of James Randi debunking various so-called "paranormal" happenings.

I mention all this to explain why I'd done little more than scan Mongfind's descriptions of various occult practices and ceremonies. And to offer some insight into my reaction when ó Cuinn said, "You should read the spells more carefully."

"Why?"

"Because then you'd know about the one I've cast tonight."

I smirked. Perhaps it wasn't polite, maybe it was rude and condescending, but I couldn't avoid it. "You cast one of the spells in Mongfind's manuscript?"

"Yes."

"I hope it was something on how to brew beer."

He answered only by nodding at the covered window. "Pull up the blinds."

What the fuck?

I almost refused. I almost got up and left, whatever was outside be damned. ó Cuinn was playing with me, and I've never been much for games.

"Why should I?"

"Because it'll make the rest of what I have to tell you easier to believe."

Or it'll give me the power to tell you, Conor, that I'm out of here and don't want to hear from you again. I reached out and grabbed the cord that controlled the blinds and pulled.

The blinds drew up—and beyond the glass, outside in the night, something was peering in at me. The face was so white the skin was slightly blue, the ears were long and with pointed tips poking up through lank, pale hair, and the corners of the thing's grin reached all the way to the bottom of those ears. The teeth were jagged and sharp, the eyes red.

It vanished almost instantly, but it'd been enough to send me up out of the chair and stumbling back. ó Cuinn leapt to his feet and moved behind me, whether to steady me or keep me from running I wasn't sure.

"It's all right, it won't hurt you," he said.

I turned to look at him. He was confident, even smug. "You're going to tell me that was the spell...?"

"Yes. I summoned the *sidh*."

"The *sidh*..." I'm sure my mouth must have fallen open for a second, in disbelief. An esteemed archaeologist was standing here, in a well-lit, modern office in the 21st century, trying to tell me that he'd performed an ancient magic ritual and had called down the *sidh*—the Little People, the Good Neighbors...*fairies*. "That's ridiculous."

"Then what did you hear outside? What did you see just now?"

As I stared at him, his gaunt, stubbled cheeks and sunken eyes and shock of coal-colored hair, I wondered: What was he trying to do? Why had he tried to scare me? Was this about to become a pitch to finance some project of his? It wasn't uncommon for people who only knew me through my work to assume that I was pagan; that I believed in the things I wrote fiction about. Was ó Cuinn pagan and thinking I was a fellow believer? Or had he thought maybe he could scam me?

"What is it you want?"

He looked genuinely perplexed (I wondered if he was just a good actor), then he said, "I want you to understand. It's very important that you do."

"Understand what?"

"What Mongfind has left us. What your role in this is."

Was he coming on to me? That notion forced me to stifle a shudder. "What if I say I don't want a role in...whatever this is?"

"You will, when you see what we have a chance to do. And you and I are the only ones who can do it, because we're the last Druids."

Now this had taken on such epic proportions of lunacy that I openly laughed. "We're Druids...you and I..."

"Yes. Think of what a Druid was: Someone who studied Celtic ways for years, who stood apart because of the specialized knowledge they possessed, who could create something from nothing."

"If I could create something from nothing, I'd have a lot more zeroes on the amount in my checking account."

"What do you do whenever you write? What else is fiction but a form of magic?"

That stopped me, because it was something that even I—the hard-bitten skeptic—believed. Even if I accepted that writing was just neurons in my brain firing, an immensely sophisticated organic computer transforming tiny electrical sparks into thoughts, thoughts that my fingers then translated into letters, it felt like magic, and I was the magician, creating (from nothing) whole worlds that would eventually be shared by others. Yes, writing was a form of magic, and a powerful one at that...but I wasn't about to believe that my ability to tell stories somehow made me a priestess for a long-dead people.

But Conor believed that. Absolutely and without question, he believed that he and I were Druids and that he (we) could perform spells that would create more than just words on paper. I had a moment then of pity for him; I could only imagine he must have been a lonely and lost man.

I looked down at his left hand, and saw that he wore a simple gold band. "Are you married?"

He blinked in surprise. "I was. My wife died three years ago. A rare form of cancer. We had six weeks after she was diagnosed." He turned the laptop towards me so I could see the desktop photo, which showed a fair-haired young woman, a baby, and a Conor who was not just younger, but almost a completely different man, with a fuller face and bright, almost kind eyes. ó Cuinn had been hollowed out by grief.

"You have a child?"

He nodded, and the smile that touched his lips made me want to like him, despite my misgivings. "Alec. He's five now; I brought him with me, to America. He's in our temporary apartment just a mile from here, with a student I hired to help me look after him."

I started walking toward the door, letting him know I was done here. "Go spend time with your little boy. I don't know why you're trying to scare me—" He started to protest, but I cut him off, raising my voice as I went on, "—but we're done. I don't think you really need me for this project anyway."

I left and he didn't stop me; but when I reached the hall, he stepped out behind me and called, "Try one of the spells yourself. That's all I ask."

I stopped and turned, ready to respond with some quick sarcastic remark, but all I could manage was, "That's crazy. Really. The Druids have been gone for fifteen hundred years, and they were really just tree-huggers, not magicians."

I walked out then. I'd convinced myself that Conor had some confederate who'd followed me before and who'd popped up outside the window. I hadn't really seen the face for more than an instant, and it could have been a mask, or even a complete fake head. I knew whoever was working with him was probably still outside, but I'd be less polite if they tried to follow me again.

Curious, though, I did walk to the point where Conor's office window faced out, and tried to examine the area beneath it. There were bushes masking the ground and the brick wall, and the growth was certainly thick enough to conceal someone crouching down. "Oh, and by the way—fuck you, too," I said, before turning to walk away.

I made it back to my car without incident and drove home still percolating with anger. By the time I crawled into bed, I'd decided that in the morning I would call Wilson Armitage and talk to him about Conor ó Cuinn.

October 23
-
October 24

When I called Dr. Armitage's office in the morning, a male voice I didn't recognize answered. "Yes?"

"Hi, this is Lisa Morton calling for Dr. Armitage."

"What did you need to speak to him about?"

Something about the voice was wrong—it was too gruff, too harsh to belong to anyone who worked at a university. "I was consulting with him on a project."

"Well, Ms. Morton, I'm afraid I have some bad news: Dr. Armitage is dead. My name's Lieutenant John Bertocelli, and I'm investigating his death."

Oh god. "How did he die?"

"He was found here on campus last night. It looks like he was attacked by some sort of wild animal, but we're not ruling out murder yet."

Wild animal...maybe something with a too-wide mouthful of jagged fangs, something that moved unseen through the night...

And I'd been there. If they found that out, would I be a suspect? Would it look better for me if I told them now? "I was at the campus last night."

"What time would that have been?"

"I came to talk to Dr. Armitage's associate Conor ó Cuinn. I was there from about eight-thirty to not quite nine."

"We think that's about the time Dr. Armitage was killed."

"Something followed me last night."

There was a pause, and I imagined the detective waving his partner over, or grabbing a notepad. "You mean something followed you last night while you were on the school grounds?"

"Yes."

"But you didn't see it?"

"No. I'm sorry."

"Don't be. If you'd gotten a look at it, you'd probably be dead today instead of Dr. Armitage." He asked a few more brief questions, then took my contact information and hung up.

After several seconds of just sitting, staring, and wondering if Conor had killed him, I googled UCLA news and found a brief mention on a local news website of Armitage's death. It didn't add much to what I'd already heard from Lt. Bertocelli—that he'd been found dead outside Haines Hall late last night, his body mauled and covered with what looked like bite marks.

That could have been me.

Maybe I'd been wrong about the face I'd seen outside the window. Maybe it'd been an animal; a mountain lion? A maddened, injured dog? Yet Conor had known it was there.

Had Conor meant to kill Wilson Armitage? Why?

I was interviewed by Lt. Bertocelli a day later, in an ugly little office with scratched furniture and sickly-green walls in a Westside police station. They told me they were still leaning toward wild animal attack, but they had some questions...mainly about Dr. Conor ó Cuinn. Apparently he and Armitage had argued earlier in the day, about something to do with what was now being called "the Celtic manuscript." Students who'd overheard the confrontation mentioned a loud "Yes, I do intend to try it," in Conor's accent, to which Armitage responded, "You can't be serious."

The fact that I'd been with ó Cuinn at the time of Wilson's death—it'd been put fairly precisely at 8:40—ruled him out as a suspect. And they told me repeatedly I was not a suspect.

They also said they might have more questions.

That night, a mountain lion was spotted in wealthy Bel Air, just to the north of the UCLA campus. It happens sometimes—

predators are driven down out of the few remaining patches of Southern California wilderness by hunger, thirst, wildfires...maybe loneliness. In another few hours, the story would probably end the way these stories always did: Some cop would claim his dart gun had jammed, and he'd just kill the poor cat instead. Meanwhile, we'd all know: That the cop, when faced with a 140-pound, yellow-eyed carnivore, had reacted on the most primeval level possible, that his every instinct had said "Kill or die," and he'd opted for the gun that he knew would put the beast down permanently. An armed caveman.

The news was already speculating that the big cat had savaged Wilson Armitage. Bel Air was within (human) walking distance of UCLA, separated only by Sunset Boulevard. It might provide a convenient close to the case.

But I knew a mountain lion was not what I'd heard following me. And it certainly wasn't the grinning, red-eyed specter I'd seen outside ó Cuinn's window.

October 27

Soon, I was too busy to think much more about Wilson Armitage and Conor ó Cuinn. I had signings to attend, interviews to give, and blog posts to write for friends. There were Halloween haunts to visit, decorations to photograph, and stores to shop in. I have a soft spot for cheap, completely useless Halloween kitsch that makes me laugh. I imagine the laborers at the manufacturing plant in China slaving over miniature Halloween skateboards and goblin finger puppets, and thinking that all Americans must surely be mad.

Then an e-mail arrived, with a generic name from a Gmail account. I almost dismissed it instantly as spam, but the subject heading read "Samhain query."

Don't open it, was my first thought.

But of course I did open it.

It was from Conor ó Cuinn. The gmail account suggested he was probably still under suspicion, and had sent this from some public computer. It was a simple message:

"Scroll to page 147 in Armitage's translation. Read the next ten pages. And remember what I said about us being the last Druids."

I wanted to delete it and forget about it. I considered telling o'Cuinn not to contact me again. Maybe I should send it to my new detective friend Bertolucci.

Instead, I opened the Mongfind translation file.

Page 147 started by recounting the moment when the Celts realized their new Catholic friends were actually an invasion force, bent on conquest. The initial attacks took out many in the warrior caste; the survivors were trying to rally their forces. And so they called on Mongfind:

> I saw our dead, our dying, our wounded. These men had now revealed that they came with no purpose other than to slay us and subjugate us. My people turned to their Arch-Druids—Mog Roith and I—in this hour of need.
>
> I sought out Mog Roith, and yet he was nowhere to be found. Our path was clear: we had to invoke the Dagda and the Morrigan and take them within ourselves. Only they would be powerful enough to lead the opposition.
>
> We searched quickly, but came to believe that Mog Roith must already be dead, although he had not been found among the corpses yet. Finally, we could tarry no longer—we had to hope the Morrigan alone would be enough.
>
> And so, protected by a ring of our strongest remaining warriors, I performed the ritual to call forth the Morrigan. Fortunately, the year was close to Samhain, and the Morrigan was near at this time.
>
> She answered my summons, and filled me. Her power! Her strength, her resolution gave me fresh hope. Sharing your body with a god is one of the most ecstatic experiences for any Druid; it is neither possession nor loss, but is instead a bonding that exceeds anything experienced by ordinary men and women. It is one of the ultimate rewards to the years of training and learning the Druid must undergo. It is among the holiest of our rites, and may be practiced only by the male and female Arch-Druids.
>
> The invocation was accomplished quickly and successfully. The Morrigan, instantly awake and aware within me, began issuing orders to our

soldiers. Then she took a spear and shield, and led them to the battlefield.

I felt everything with her, as we cut a bloody swath through the opposing troops. Our speed and skill were unmatched. The first row of enemies went down beneath spear thrusts and a shield wielded as a second weapon. Gore soaked us; we shook it from our eyes and kept going, bloodlust increasing our power. We raged through their ranks, and behind us the Celtic warriors were renewed, screaming their battle cries. The invaders began to panic; many tried to run, only to collide with their comrades behind them. Our shield sprouted arrows like deadly quills, but nothing could harm us. We were invincible. We would win.

Eire would remain ours forever.

But then the enemy forces began to scatter for another reason—something was coming up from behind them, something they *wanted* to let through. The Morrigan and I sensed an intelligence approaching, familiar and usually welcomed…

The last of their rows parted, and Mog Roith stepped through; Mog is blind, but because he moved among the soldiers easily, I knew that the Dagda had joined him and given him sight.

"Mongfind," he said—except "Morrigan" impossibly came from his mouth at the same time—"we must cease this fighting."

I felt the Morrigan's disbelief surge through me, and I shared it. The Dagda and the Morrigan were the great defenders of Eire; they'd fought against Fomorians and *sidh*, they were the most valorous warriors of the *Tuatha de Danaan*. The Dagda would never call for an end to defending our land.

"No," the Morrigan and I answered, "we must drive them out."

Mog Roith smiled, sadly…and then raised the great club he held and brought it down on our head.

> When I awakened, a day later, the Morrigan was gone, I was bound and gagged in a dank cell, and I knew the invaders had won.
>
> Eire was theirs.
>
> Mog Roith had betrayed us. He had summoned the Dagda and then used the god's power against us. I never found out why, I never knew what the Catholics and their God could possibly have offered. I did find out that shortly after he bludgeoned me, he staggered from the battlefield to an oak grove, took a sacred knife and slit his own throat. Or, likely, the furious Dagda took over and repaid Mog Roith's betrayal. One may partner with the gods, but one cannot betray them and expect the forged bond not to shatter.

I'd read this account earlier, but hadn't really looked at what followed it: Instructions for performing the ritual to invoke the spirit of the Morrigan. It was a comparatively simple procedure, requiring none of the paraphernalia (a rod made of ash, a wand fashioned from an oak twig) of most of the other spells I'd glanced at. Fasting was suggested, but I knew Mongfind had performed it successfully without that; the rest consisted of assuming a posture known as the Heron Stance, and meditating while inciting an invocation. It reiterated that only a female Arch-Druid could successfully invoke the Morrigan.

I had no idea why ó Cuinn wanted me to read this passage. Yes, the account of Mongfind laying into her Catholic enemies while possessed by a goddess was stirring fiction, but what did any of this have to do with me? Did ó Cuinn actually believe that he and I were Arch-Druids?

I tried to focus on writing an article I had promised an online news site, but my thoughts kept circling back to ó Cuinn's suggestion. It was ludicrous; the thought of me standing in the middle of my living room floor, one foot braced against the opposite knee, trying to keep my balance while reciting words that sounded like a Lewis Carroll poem…I couldn't foresee that ending with anything but me collapsing onto the carpet, cursing my own innate clumsiness.

Still…what could it hurt? It wasn't as if this ritual required the sacrifice of a child, or even a blood oath. Fifteen minutes of my time, and it might be an interesting experiment; perhaps it would help me to understand, at least in some small part, how ecstatic states could be reached in shamanistic practices. Maybe I'd feel a little of what Mongfind had felt, nearly two millennia ago. Maybe I'd understand how she could have possibly believed that she'd been in communion with a goddess.

The chant was simple[14]; it only took me a few seconds to memorize it. I stood, walked to a clear space in my living room, raised one leg, and tried to concentrate.

The first few seconds were disastrous. I wobbled; I lost the pose; I laughed; I almost returned to my desk, thankful that no one had been around to witness my attempt.

But instead I opted to remain as serious as possible; I was, as I mentioned, curious about the state it would theoretically produce in the practitioner.

I held the pose, one leg bent, the foot resting against the other knee, thinking about engravings I'd seen of Celtic warriors in this pose, and Australian aborigines…and after a time of struggling to stay upright, my difficulties seemed to fall away and were replaced with calm steadiness. My eyes closed, the chant continued to flow past my lips, becoming more effortless with each recitation. With every passing second, it became easier to concentrate solely on the words…the invitation…

Awareness seemed to simultaneously fall away and expand. I was calm, focused…open.

Something was in the room with me. I felt it like a blanket, or like a luxurious wrap made of the most exquisite fabric. It was warmth, and strength, and comfort. I didn't open my eyes,

[14] I'm not including the actual chant here because...well, even though it can supposedly be performed only by a Druid priest or priestess of the highest level; let's just say I nonetheless have some safety concerns. Don't try this at home, in other words.

because there was no need; there was nothing in this sensation to alarm me, to cause anxiety or dread.

The chant continued, and so did the presence. It enveloped me; it spoke without words, telling me it—or, rather, she, because there was something quintessentially feminine about this presence—had come at my bidding. The no-words conveyed admiration and love, and surprise, because it had been millennia since she had been thus called.

The Morrigan.

At this point, my skepticism was laid to rest by desire—I wanted nothing more than to join with this power, to feel it within me, infusing me. I wanted nothing so badly as to feel what Mongfind had felt, as she'd strode onto a battlefield without fear, striking down her foes with grace and divine skill.

The warmth was inside me, then, and…

October 27

Time Unknown

...First are the smells, my head is flooded not just with the scent of cooking meat from the apartment below but the half-wrapped chocolate bar I left on my desk, the jasmine soap from the bathroom and the odd chemical tang of dishwashing liquid and detergent from the kitchen (and how is it possible I've never noticed before how intense that is and how it grates), I can feel every fiber of the carpet beneath my bare feet and the air on the skin of my arms and face and the sounds—so many, so loud—the sounds of music thumping from somewhere nearby, a helicopter whup-whup-whupping overhead and a bass rumble which it takes me several seconds to identify as my own heartbeat and I still taste the wine I drank an hour ago and the brightness of my computer screen nearly forces me to turn my head away but it's glorious, a fire that glows unlike any we've seen before-and it is "we" now, because I share these wonders with another who has fit into me like a sleek hand into a glove, I can feel the energy she brings with her throbbing and pushing fire through my limbs and she tests them, moves my arms and then my legs and we're outside, running through the October night, no shoes but it doesn't matter because nothing can hurt us, not the speeding cars that we leap away from, clearing the hood of a parked truck as easily as stepping over a bump in the ground, we run, reveling in the rush of our own blood as it flows through muscles that she has made flexible and fit, it's not just the particle-thickened Los Angeles air we can feel on our flesh and within our lungs, but we can feel the veil, too, the membrane that separates our worlds, we can almost glimpse what lies beyond it, the grimacing *sidh* and the shadowy dead ones, the things with shifting form like smoke and with black hearts that seek to suck and devour, and we see how thin that veil is, because it's almost the end of the month (of summer, and of the year), it's only a few nights from Samhain, when that skin will be thinnest, and one with craft—one like a Druid—could reach past, yet that world doesn't interest us right now because we've heard something coming from one of the intersecting streets ahead of us, a voice raised in anger, and that tone reacts within her like a flammable chemical set on fire so we follow, moving so quickly that the houses and apartment complexes and parked cars are a blur, we run three blocks to where the buildings are a little older, a little more in need of repair, and coming from a bottom-floor apartment is the voice of a man shouting obscenities at a woman, who offers nothing but weak, sobbing responses, and we draw closer, standing outside the door of the apartment, listening, and something within crashes and shatters, and the woman cries out, and then the door is flying open (it was so easy to break its flimsy lock), and there's a man, young, heavyset, wearing a stained T-shirt, drawing back a fist, but the woman is already bleeding from the nose, her eyes wide as she sees us, and he turns and swings at us instead; we catch the blow and laugh at the expression on his face as we squeeze his hand, grinding the fingers against each other until he screams; we force him down while the woman stands back, silent now, staring in disbelief; with our other hand we strike him again, in the temple, and he wobbles but doesn't fall, and I know one more blow will kill him and we're pulling back our arm a second time, and I know I can stop this now, I can take control and we can leave, return home before we take this man's life, leave him to prey upon her until she dies at 28 or 32 or (unlikely) 40, beaten down and used up, but I don't stop it, I want to feel this happening, to rid the world of this abuser and to know what death feels like; so I let her draw back our fist and bring it down again and this time his eyes roll up and he falls like a butchered steer, and we can no longer hear his breath or his heart so we know he's dead, and we turn to the woman, and I understand that by tomorrow she will describe us as a male, six feet tall and tattooed, and we turn to leave, half-drunk on violence, and *her* influence is ebbing as she takes us home again on middle-aged legs that pump now with a failing rhythm, as we reach home I notice the blood on my fingers and the panic I feel is mine alone and she leaves then, and in that instant, when all that she brought with her is suddenly taken from me, my legs give way and my eyes lose focus and…

October 28

Day

...The first thing I noticed when I woke up in the morning was how much my hands hurt.

Then I realized I'd fallen asleep fully dressed on the couch in the living room. I sat up, aching from the cushions, bleary-eyed, blinking against morning sun. I raised a hand to rub away the sleep—and saw the blood crusted across my fingers.

I...*we*...killed a man last night.

The memories washed through me, a toxic rain poisoning whatever it touched. I remembered all of it.

Or did I?

I ran to my computer and googled "North Hollywood Crime News." The search took me to a local news station's updates...and there it was, under the headline "NORTH HOLLYWOOD MAN FOUND DEAD BY ABUSED WIFE, SUSPECT SOUGHT." They were looking for a male, approximately six feet tall, medium build, brown hair.

It had happened. Exactly as I remembered it, down to the Morrigan using her influence to guarantee the wife's unwitting complicity.

There was something else there: Last night, I'd apparently typed the account of the possession, while it was still fresh.[15] I had only a vague memory of doing it, in some sort of dreamlike state.

---

[15] The previous chapter was exactly what I found on my computer.

I ran to the bathroom, turned on the shower, and stepped in, still clothed. There wasn't much blood on me—mainly on my hand, and some of that was mine—but I still planned on washing these clothes after, then driving to some distant dumpster and disposing of them.

As the hot water flooded over me, turning pink when it swirled around the drain, I began to remember more. The Morrigan had left me with thoughts tucked away, thoughts I pulled forth as I relaxed beneath the steady warmth:

I saw, clearly, an archaic, idyllic settlement, perched on a green hill. Spacious houses built of wood and stone clustered about a palace ornamented in gold; I recognized the geometric spiral ornamentation as Celtic in origin. Smoke curled from a hundred chimneys, the people wore heavy torques over fine robes, and they glowed with health and happiness. I understood that an old man, still hardy, his white beard and a few wrinkles the only clues to his longevity, was more than 150 years old. I saw a school where young men and women studied history and lore, and I felt a strange kinship with them.

This was Mongfind's world, before the invaders came.

Another memory appeared in my mind's eye, and I saw a Samhain ritual. A great cake was prepared, cut into small portions, and one portion was rubbed with charcoal on the bottom. Warriors and young nobles lined up to choose pieces, and when a handsome young man turned his over to find the blackened underside, he smiled and received the congratulations of those around him. At night, the Druids led him to a pond; there, as he stood quietly, dressed in the finest jewels and raiments, they began the Samhain ritual. Mongfind and Mog Roith used chalk dust to draw a protective circle around those present, while they invoked sanctuary. First, the two Arch-Druids offered a black sheep; they moved in perfect, long-practiced unity, and the animal died almost instantly. Then, with great dignity, Mongfind knotted a rope about the neck of the handsome young man as she chanted a prayer to Bal-Sab, the Lord of Death. At a signal from her, the sacrifice knelt by the side of the bog, his expression serene. Mog Roith stepped up, and while she tightened the noose, her male counterpart thrust a ceremonial dagger into the young man's chest; then, together, they pushed his head down beneath the waters of the bog. He was, in effect, simultaneously hanged, stabbed, and drowned, satisfying the classic Druidical obsession with the number three.

With the sacrifices completed, a weight filled the air. The fires ringing the bog darkened; even Mongfind was plainly unnerved.

Bal-sab had come.

I felt Mongfind's anxiety as she waited with the others. The air literally thickened, pressurized; one young man's knees buckled and he sank to the soggy ground, gasping. A noxious odor arose, the scent of spilled blood and decayed corpses. Mongfind fought back an urge to gag, then withdrew her own knife, ready to offer herself should the protective circle prove insufficient.

Seconds passed like small eternities. The future hung on this void; if it found the offerings unworthy, it could release horrors beyond death on the people. Mongfind offered up silent prayers to the other gods, but this was Bal-sab's moment.

The dark god's overpowering presence vanished abruptly, and the gathered Druids all exhaled in relief. Bal-sab had accepted the sacrifices, and ensured another year of prosperity for his worshippers. A feast would commence now, and even if the *sidh* should cross over, Mongfind and Mog Roith would be ready. The Celts would enjoy another year of prosperity, until next Samhain.

Samhain...Halloween...four days away.

I finished the shower, dressed, walked to the living room on legs gone numb, didn't even correct myself when I missed the couch and sagged to the floor.

True. All of it, true.

The Morrigan had possessed me last night, and together we'd committed murder. I'd just washed our victim's blood from my hands, and yet that wasn't what had taken the feeling from me and dropped me:

I couldn't deny what had happened last night—any of it. There was a world beyond ours—a world of violent gods and ancient magic and hunger for human life. History is a lie and reality a thin sheet, beyond which we sometimes glimpse shadows that strut and grasp at us. Nothing in Mongfind's journal was fantasy or deception; it was the truth, not what I'd spent my life experiencing and believing.

And ó Cuinn…he'd known exactly which spell to send me to, the one that would provide an encounter so intimate that even the most confirmed of skeptics wouldn't deny it. This couldn't be explained away as a cheap Halloween mask, or even the finest special effects trick created by a master wizard.

Or could it?

I still couldn't accept it completely. A drug, perhaps; certain psychotropics were widely used to induce ecstatic states. Could ó Cuinn have somehow slipped me something? I thought back to everything I'd eaten and drunk yesterday—tea from my own supply, Thai food from the same restaurant I ate at twice a week, wine from a bottle I'd just opened. It didn't seem likely, but…

What if he hadn't tampered with my food? That meant he was right—that we were both Druids, that he had called up the *sidh*…

That they'd murdered Wilson Armitage.

Had ó Cuinn meant that to happen? Or had he been unable to control his guests once they'd arrived here?

After some time I found the strength to rise, and resolved to continue with my schedule as planned. I'd taken this week off from my day job as a bookseller to focus on my Halloween commitments, and I wouldn't abandon those now. I had a phone interview set up with the BBC in thirty minutes—I'd be damned if I'd give that up now because I'd had a psychedelic trip into fairyland.

Even as I thought that, I hoped I wouldn't be damned for other reasons.

October 28

Evening

I managed to get through the day somehow. In between interviews and answering e-mails, I packed last night's clothes into a trash bag, drove to an alley thirty minutes away, found an open dumpster, tossed the bag in and came home again.

Night fell, and I drove to Dark Delicacies, a nearby genre specialty bookstore, for a signing. I didn't like the idea of being out at night, but this wouldn't be like walking across a large, empty campus; even if I had to park a short distance from the store, I'd be walking past stores on a heavily-trafficked street.

The signing was pleasant if under-attended (aren't they all), and afterward I ended up walking with friends to a coffee shop two blocks away, where we gabbed over tea and dessert. For an hour or so, I was able to forget about goddesses and murder and pagan rituals, as we lost ourselves in the simple, mundane pleasures of gossip and jokes.

At 11 p.m. (how had it gotten to be that late?), the shop closed up and kicked us out, we said our goodbyes on the sidewalk, and I turned to head for my car, now parked several blocks away. It was late enough that the stores had closed, and few cars drove by. In the distance I could hear the ever-present sound of sirens (in an area as big as L.A., there's always a catastrophe happening somewhere) and the thrum of freeway congestion.

I came to an intersection, and even though I couldn't see any approaching cars, I waited for the crosswalk light to turn green—

the last thing in the world I needed right now was for a hidden cop to nab me for jaywalking.

"I'm really sorry, officer, and—what? No, that's not blood under my fingernails, of course not..." My rational mind assured me that there was no visible blood beneath the nails of the hands I'd scrubbed until they were raw and red, but I still wasn't taking any chances. I waited.

The shop on the corner was one of those little cluttered gift shops, the kind that you glance in and you can't imagine buying any of this kitschy nonsense and you wonder how they stay in business. Because it was Halloween, their front display windows were full of little papier mâché pumpkins (some were sprayed with glitter or even wore little aprons, which offended my highly-honed sense of Halloween decorum), cute witch and cat figurines, and gingerbread-scented candles. There were Halloween salt shakers and mugs and hand towels.

Near the bottom was a jack-o'-lantern that made me stop and stare. It was white, almost the size of a real pumpkin, and lit with some sort of reddish glow from within. It also bore one of the most grotesquely carved faces I'd ever seen—eyes with knitted brows, a huge snaggletoothed grin, and two slits for a nose. It didn't begin to match the other items in the window, all of which would have been more at home in an Anne Geddes photo book than a Stephen King novel, and it was the only piece that seemed to be lit.

I was bending down to look more closely at it when it moved. It turned and looked directly up at me.

Now I knew why it looked familiar. I'd seen it before, outside the window of ó Cuinn's office.

But this time it didn't vanish abruptly—I think it wanted me to see it. Its rictus grin widened, spilling even more crimson light out around it, although I couldn't make out the rest of its body. I took one, two steps back—

HOONNNK! I'd backed right into the street, and hadn't even noticed the car barreling through the intersection. Heart hammering, I leapt back up onto the curb and the car sped off into the night.

When I looked back at the window, the face was gone.

It was coming for me.

Fuck it—I ran, then, ran against the red light and regardless of who might see me and wonder what I was running from. I didn't look into any of the other windows I passed, or listen for the sound of tiny footsteps coming up behind me, closer and closer...I ran, digging into my purse as I neared my car, trying to find my keys which always fell to the bottom of the voluminous bag, requiring precious extra seconds to dig them out—

I had them. I flipped up the car key, jammed it into the lock, threw the door open, and fell into the front seat. I slammed the door behind me, pressed the lock button—and flinched as something hit the door outside hard, making the whole car shake. I heard a high-pitched squeal.

Somehow I managed to get the right key into the ignition, start the car, and take off, burning rubber. I'd driven two blocks before I realized the parking brake was still on. I ran one stoplight (got lucky), then risked a glance in the rearview mirror.

Nothing but a quiet street of closed shops. A few headlights in the distance. Nothing chasing me, no sign of anything unusual.

Five minutes later I was home. I waited a few moments before I opened the car door—what if it had somehow attached itself to the car, or followed where I couldn't see it? Did it even need normal laws of physics? Could it simply wish itself here, to continue its mischief...or worse?

When it proved quiet, I opened the door and stepped out. Still safe. Closing the door, I glanced down—and saw a dent in the door panel.

So much for the drugged theory.

I walked, fast, to my front door, got in, closed it behind me and checked all the locks, then collapsed onto the couch. I'm not used to adrenaline rushes, and I was surprised to realize I was shaking. My little tortoiseshell cat, Roxie, helped by sitting at my ankles and mewing at me in gentle concern. The simple act of stroking her warm back and feeling her purr beneath my touch calmed me. We sometimes forget the power of the most common acts, don't we? This ancient communion with another species, something that has been part of human life for thousands of years, was its own kind of magic, with a peculiar power to restore and heal.

The phone rang, jarring me from my brief peace. I got up, stepped around Roxie, and checked caller ID—it was Ricky, calling from North Carolina.

Hearing his voice was another gift, but—after exchanging the usual greetings—his message was disturbing. "I had the strangest thing happen tonight, and I knew you'd appreciate this."

The film had put their cast and crew up in a nice hotel in downtown Wilmington. Ricky had a room on the fifth floor, and we'd already joked about how they called the view from his window "Cape Fear Riverfront." It was too bad he wasn't making a horror movie.

"I had this nice dinner tonight with a couple of guys from the crew—we found this little seafood place you'd love—and then I came up to my room. I was just getting ready for bed when I thought I heard something on the other side of the window, so I looked—and there was some kind of strange face out there. I only got a glimpse of it before it disappeared. It must have been one of the guys punking me, because they know about you and Halloween—at least that's all I can figure."

Cold rushed through me, freezing me to the spot. "What did this face look like?"

"Well, that was kind of the giveaway: It looked like a jack-o'-lantern. I figure they probably picked up one of those battery-operated things that are in all the stores right now and lowered it down on a line. In fact, it was probably Dave from Effects—he's been teasing me all week."

A jack-o'-lantern. Of course. It was so obvious, and yes I'd missed it—they looked too much like malevolent, glowing jack-o'-lanterns for it to be sheer coincidence.

"Hon…you there?"

"Sorry. Long day. You're not going out again tonight, right?"

"No. Why?"

What could I say? That what he'd seen hadn't been a cheap Halloween prop; that he was being threatened by otherworldly forces because of me? Because of something that an Irish archaeologist in Los Angeles had unleashed? Something that pulverized the well-ordered, rational world we both believed in…or at least, used to believe in?

And then there was his job—this film was important to both of us. It was a good supporting role in a serious movie, with a young writer/director who we liked and admired. And, frankly, the money would make our lives much easier. If I told him now I was in trouble, he'd leave the movie and come home. We couldn't afford that…and frankly, I wasn't ready to involve him in this. There was only one person who could help, and I would need to deal with him alone.

"Just be careful."

"Are you okay?" He knew me too well, and his warmth thawed the chill that had paralyzed me.

"Yeah, I'm fine. Just another long day."

We spent the rest of the call talking about my signing, the interview I'd given today to a Montreal radio station, a nice customer review that had gone up at Amazon for my book. We said the things that parted lovers have said to each other, in letters, on phones, in text messages, for centuries. Then we hung up.

I checked the locks again, risked a glance outside, and decided to try to sleep, even though I knew it was unlikely. And if I did…would my dreams leave me more exhausted and unsettled in the morning?

October 29

A strange whining sound from Roxie woke me in the morning.

It was earlier than my usual waking time, but the sun was already up, and I was surprised to realize I had slept.

But that sound—I'd never heard her make anything like it. She was in the living room, so I couldn't see (or imagine) what would have caused her to act that way. "Roxie?"

She didn't stop—she sounded almost like a small child uttering a string of nonsense syllables. The sound brought last night's unease hurtling back, but the fact that it was already light outside was reassuring.

I got out of bed, ventured into the living room—and saw instantly what had provoked the sound from my cat:

Outside, on my enclosed, second-floor balcony, a large carved pumpkin rested. The jack-o'-lantern's face was a small masterwork of carving skill, exuding vicious glee.

I picked up Roxie, trying to calm her, and together we stared at the sinister objet d'art beyond the glass. After a few seconds, I saw that the shadow around the base of the pumpkin wasn't just dark. It was dark red, and thick.

The thing was oozing blood. And as I knelt so I could see through its empty grin, I saw there was something inside, something with fur.

Whatever was in there wasn't moving, but it was still bleeding. The thin shape just visible through one eye socket might have been a tail, a pointed extension was possibly an ear.

A cat. Maybe still alive. Probably not, but...

If it was still alive, I couldn't stand there and watch it bleed out. Yes, Ripley went back for the cat in Alien, and I'd risk a dangerous encounter now to check on an animal that wasn't even mine. That's one of the things about compassion—it trumps both fear and common sense.

Because I knew, at that moment, exactly what I was confronting. There was no question that the jack-o'-lantern and the bloodied animal were not the work of ordinary pranksters. For one thing, my balcony is difficult to reach, accessible only by going through my living room or coming down from the apartment building's roof. The pumpkin was a large one, and would have been hard for even a strong man to carry down a ladder. And I didn't want to accept that any humans were capable of inflicting gruesome harm on a small animal and then stuffing its corpse into a hollowed-out squash.

No, I trusted then that if I stepped outside, I might be facing vicious, inhuman things.

I locked Roxie in the bedroom, then went to the hallway closet and found the baseball bat stored there. It was a good, solid wooden Louisville Slugger, and had been given to me years ago as a gift after I'd called the police on a psycho who'd threatened a friend with it. It had heft to it, and gave me enough confidence to slide the glass door open and step out onto the balcony.

It was still early, but the day was already warm and clear, and it was hard to believe anything more threatening than a hungry squirrel would be nearby. I was guessing the *sidh* moved at night and had left this before vanishing at dawn, but I didn't know that for sure.

And...there might be something hurt and alive inside the pumpkin.

I used the bat to reach down and knock the pumpkin's top aside. A smell assaulted me, a thick, musky odor that I knew from an emergency visit to a veterinarian to fix an injured cat: The smell of fear and feline blood.

I bent over the pumpkin and looked in. I could see there was a small animal within: black, unmoving. A black cat. I poked at it tentatively with the bat, but there was no response. I went back in for a heavy towel and then returned. I laid the towel by the pumpkin, picked it up gingerly, and tilted the cat out onto the towel.

Now it was clear: It was dead. Its throat had been slit. Gore matted its soft black fur.

I understood then how the *sidh* had earned their reputation as savage pranksters: A black cat was not just a classic Halloween icon, it was also the source of one of the most common urban legends: that Satanic cults kidnapped black cats every Halloween and sacrificed them in diabolical rituals. There was no basis to that story whatsoever.

Until now, that is.

The *sidh* had slain an innocent cat to taunt me. The message was clear, and my response would be as well.

I took little comfort from the fact that I didn't know this cat—it didn't belong to a neighbor, it wasn't a local stray I'd glimpsed from time to time. I wrapped up the small corpse in the towel and placed it in a plastic bag; later on, I'd find a nice patch of yard and bury it. I'd deal with the pumpkin and the blood later. I had something more important to do now.

I found ó Cuinn's phone number and called him.

He answered on the first ring, and sounded wary when he heard my voice. "The little friends you called up are stalking me," I told him.

"Can we meet somewhere?"

I knew he was worried about the police still possibly tracking him, but right then I didn't give two fucks about him or the cops. "No. Just reverse this shit, Conor. I don't care what it takes, get rid of them. Now."

There was a pause before he answered, "I can't."

"What do you mean—you can't, or you won't?"

"I mean, I can't. Look at the manuscript yourself—the banishing spell is only partial. That section of the manuscript is illegible."

"You're kidding." I paced my living room, wishing I could reach through the phone and strangle ó Cuinn. "You called these things up before making sure you could get rid of them?"

"I...I really didn't think they'd be a problem. What exactly are they...what—"

I cut him off. "They left a dead, mutilated cat on my balcony this morning, just for starters."

"Are you sure it wasn't the work of pranksters?"

I had to laugh at how our roles had suddenly reversed themselves: two nights ago I'd walked out on this man when he'd told me we were both Druids, and now he was arguing in favor of human mischief while I advocated for the supernatural. "I've seen them, Conor."

"Oh. Dear God. I never thought—"

I hung up on him. He was an irritating idiot. He was the fool in every bad horror movie who read the ancient spell out loud, who taunted the killer, who had sex while a madman lurked in the shadows. I'd solve this without him, then.

I brought up the manuscript on the computer, and found the banishing spell. He was right about that, at least: The beginning of it was there—it involved a rod made of ash and a spoken command—but the rest was lost.

I'd find another way, then. Could I still use logic against something that was essentially illogical? At this point, didn't it make the most sense to accept the irrational, to just acknowledge that the supernatural did exist? But could that doorway be only partly opened? If the *sidh* were real (they were), what else was behind that portal? I'd met one goddess already—how many more were there? Was there one single God, watching impassively?

Unless He was going to intervene now, I'd have to wrestle with that question later on. Right now I needed to come up with some way to fight the deadly tricksters Conor had called up. I needed to think about practical magic, not impractical theology.

I tried to remember everything I could about Samhain encounters with the *sidh,* and later Scottish stories of fairies on Halloween. A few tales talked about silver or iron; one odd legend mentioned wearing your clothes inside out. Mostly the old folklore suggested avoiding them.

I pulled down some of my reference books and flipped through them, but everything that I found described ways to protect yourself from the *sidh,* not get rid of them. Or even hurt them.

But I knew there was a way—Mongfind had recorded one, but I only had part of it. A rod of ash…a command…what else?

I glanced out my balcony at the bloody jack-o'-lantern, and the sight of it triggered a realization: The *sidh* had carved the pumpkin in a recreation of their own faces. Their heads, in fact, with the oversized, round shape and glowing features, looked like living jack-o'-lanterns.

Was it possible that the classic Halloween jack-o'-lantern—that most beloved of the holiday's symbols—had been based on the faces of the *sidh*? Or was there even more to it than simply remembering the *sidh* in folk art?

Before bringing Halloween to America[16], the Irish had carved turnips into jack-o'-lanterns. Common wisdom held that the vegetables—with a candle placed inside—had been used to startle passersby on Halloween night, but now I believed they might have served another purpose:

What if the jack-o'-lanterns had originally represented the ultimate defense against the *sidh* on Halloween night? Were they perhaps used in Mongfind's ritual? Were stories of Irish lads smashing their sculpted turnips on Halloween night indicating more than just sheer playfulness?

The baseball bat was made of ash…it would certainly be very effective in smashing a pumpkin…

Somehow I knew this was right. Maybe it was some part of the Morrigan, still residing in me; or my own intuition, telling me that the connections I'd just drawn were simply too strong.

Maybe it was Druid knowledge, buried deep within me. Magic encoded in DNA, like musical ability or language skills.

---

[16] Mainly in the mid-nineteenth century, after the Great Potato Famine devastated the food supply in Ireland.

I would wait until evening, when the *sidh* were present again. I knew I'd be putting myself in peril, but I also thought it might be the only way to banish them—would they react to a command and a banishment ritual during the day, when they didn't seem to be present?

No, I had to risk it. At sundown, I'd use the bat—my rod of ash—to shatter the pumpkin they'd left me as a cruel taunt, and I'd command them to return to their own world.

And if I was wrong and it didn't work...then come Halloween, the *sidh* would make any human terrorists look like preschoolers.

October 29

Evening

I spent the rest of the daylight hours going over Mongfind's manuscript, paying attention to the charms, spells and rituals that I'd only glanced at before.

Most of them were little more than recipes or instructions: How to prepare a tea that would cure nausea, how to make a poultice for a leg wound, how to keep berries picked in October from spoiling by November.

But then there were the more serious magicks as well. These included:

- Shapeshifting
- Communicating with the dead
- Enchanting a spear so it would never miss its target
- Creating a cup that would never empty of mead
- Traveling via an astral body
- Invisibility
- Invulnerability in battle
- Passing into the Otherworld, or the realm of the *sidh*

A few of the incantations were missing key words; despite Mongfind's precautions, parts of the manuscript had blurred with the passage time. A few sections were spattered with something dark that covered the writing—probably Mongfind's own blood, coughed out as her lungs had failed her over that long final winter.

There were some instructions on creating protective wards, in case I failed in my attempt at performing the banishing ceremony.

I should perhaps make clear that none of these practices were presented as symbolic acts; this wasn't some new age book in which transforming into a wolf meant you'd been granted a license to behave a little wildly in the sack. No, in Mongfind's book transforming into a wolf meant you grew hair, got down on four paws, and grew teeth as sharp as knife tips. This wasn't bogus spiritualism; this was the real deal.

As the sun dropped in the sky, I made sure the (now empty) jack-o'-lantern, its base stained red, was placed squarely in the center of my balcony. I moved everything—chairs, potted plants, etc.—well away, so I'd have room to swing the bat. I took down the wind chimes and the cute orange lights Ricky had strung around the eaves. Then I stepped in, closed the glass door, and waited.

Five PM...five-thirty...six, and the sun was gone. The sky overhead glowed like burnished steel, leaving the ficus and magnolia trees to stand in mute silhouette. I made sure my lights were all on, my front door locked, my bat in hand.

I hoped I wouldn't need to worry about my own cat; she'd been fed an hour earlier, and was now probably curled up on a corner of my bed, sleeping off dinner.

Or so I thought, until I heard her screaming.

The shriek was piercing, and sent me rushing into the bedroom; it sounded as if she was still on the bed, and now the cry was punctuated with hissing. I reached the bedroom—

The lights went off in the apartment.

The terrible sound of the cat's shriek redoubled.

By the light coming in through the bedroom blinds, I saw a flash of something moving around the edge of the bed.

Of course: they could come into a building. I'd been stupid to think that somehow doors and walls could keep out things that came from another dimension.

I felt my way to the apartment's breaker panel in the hall, threw back the hinged cover, and started flipping switches. The power returned, the lights came back on—

Something rushed past me, leaving the skin of my leg chilled through my jeans. I heard a high-pitched tiny cackle from the living room, echoing as if it came from the far end of a cave.

Clutching and lifting the bat, I stepped cautiously into the living room. Behind me, the cat quieted and I heard her paws hit the floor as she leapt from the bed and scurried beneath it in alarm.

Good girl.

That left me just needing to get through the living room to the sliding door, and the balcony beyond. Meaning, of course, I just had to get past what waited for me somewhere in the living room.

One step…two…

I heard something skitter behind a bookcase to my right. I edged to the left, trying to move away from it—

And heard a snicker below the couch to my left. Followed by a tiny cry from behind the desk in front of me.

There was more than one of them. In fact, they were hidden throughout the entire apartment.

One brushed against my ankles. I jumped and swung the bat, which crushed a corner of the coffee table but nothing else.

I turned, seeking them, determined to take a swing at the next little fucker who touched me.

But…

Their voices came from all around me now. They whispered together, but because there must have been dozens of them circling me the whispers became a single loud pulsing hiss.

I felt a sharp sting in my right calf, and knew I'd been bitten. I kicked backwards, but only managed to nearly throw myself off balance and go down.

How long before they'd all be on me, with their claws and jack-o'-lantern grins…

Of course: The jack-o'-lantern. They'd almost made me forget my original purpose.

I ran to the glass door and slid it open. Behind me, talons raked both ankles while they cackled in feral glee.

But they were too late; I'd reached my goal. I raised the bat and turned to face them. The lights were out again in the apartment, and through the glass I saw their eyes, glimmering, savoring what they thought was their victory.

The command was simple: I ordered them to return to their own world, and then I brought the bat down. The pumpkin caved in, spraying orange pulp in a wide circle.

The *sidh's* chortles turned to shrieks. The glow of their eyes faded. And behind them…

I saw their world, for an instant that has proven to be unforgettable: A black, starless sky looked down on a lifeless landscape. Gray, leafless trees sprouted from depthless bogs, stones sculpted into shapes like headstones with leering faces rose from mounds of soggy earth—and then the stone faces turned to leer at me. The *sidh* scuttled among it all like maggots on a rotting corpse, and before the gap between us closed, I saw from the way they glared at me that mere prank-playing wouldn't be involved should we meet again.

It was over. The lights in the apartment flickered back on, the bat dropped from my fingers into the mess of the shattered pumpkin, and the pain ignited in my legs.

I moved into the light to examine the damage they'd inflicted on me: There were three striped claw marks on my left leg, and four pinprick puncture marks on my right. They were trickling blood, although none seemed deep enough to require stitches. But…

Were the *sidh* venomous? Did they carry disease, had they succeeded in killing me in a way that would just take longer…and be even more painful?

I swabbed the wounds out in the bathroom, but stopped before bandaging them, wondering if Mongfind's writings could offer any aid. Upon checking, I found a recipe for a poultice that would cure "the bites of dangerous creatures of all kinds." It required a few herbs I didn't have, but that I thought I could find at a nearby health food market.

I put bandaids on and stepped out the door. A moment of apprehension caused me to wait halfway down the stairs, ears straining...but I was reassured by the normal night sounds: Cars, dogs barking, a neighbor's inane television sitcom.

I'd successfully performed a banishment ritual.

As I headed to the market, I felt fresh confidence, and I knew I would survive the *sidh's* wounds.

I could create and control magic, even better than Conor ó Cuinn.

I was a Druid.

I was living inside one of my own Halloween stories.

I've written two Halloween-themed novellas[17]; both are about ordinary, middle-aged adults who find themselves surrounded by ancient, malevolent supernatural forces on Halloween. In both, the protagonists fight to hang onto something: (a child, a business). In both, the fight climaxes in another world.

What was I fighting for? I wasn't fighting to protect my (dis)beliefs; they'd already been taken from me.

There was something bigger at stake. Much bigger.

But now I felt fever setting in, and I had to concentrate on making it to the market, buying what I needed, getting home and putting together Mongfind's poultices. By the time I crawled into bed, the heavy packs of herbs taped against the burning wounds, I was shaking and sweating. If Mongfind's cure didn't work, whatever else was at stake wouldn't matter, at least not to me.

---

[17] *The Samhanach* (2010) and *Hell Manor* (2012)

October 30

Before Dawn

Fever dreams:

I soar into the night sky, but instead of more stars appearing the higher I go, they disappear, one by one, then whole galaxies, and I realize something huge has reared up between me and space. Something completely black and lightless, huge and freezing.

Bal-sab. Lord of Death.

I look down, and the earth is below me, but it's no longer my earth; I'm in the past now, looking down on the ruins of the great Celtic palaces. It's Samhain, and there are no Druids left to sate Bal-sab's hunger, so he takes his sacrifice in other ways. He waves a vast limb, and the portals to the Otherworld open, releasing the *sidh.* They ravage through Europe, bringing the Black Death with them; when wise women attempt to banish them, they fester in the minds of neighbors, judges, priests and inquisitors, who torture and burn the women. The witches.

Centuries pass, and Bal-sab's voracious appetite continues unabated. He finally tires of letting the *sidh* do his dirty work, and he takes to whispering in the minds of great men, infesting their brilliance with visions of mass destruction. Those he seduces produce ever more powerful weapons: Catapults, cannons, nerve gas, nuclear bombs.

Where are the other gods? Why do they allow this?

"Because we must," answers the Morrigan, and I feel her presence beside/inside me.

"Why? Why can't you stop him?"

"He is Death. Death, more than any of us, must continue. Without Death, there would be no balance."

"But..." I struggle to find the words. "The world wasn't always like this."

The Morrigan's sadness courses through me like tears in a creased cheek. "No. And it need not be this way now."

"How?"

But I know. Even as I ask it, I know.

"Even Death can be forgiving," she says, before disappearing.

I awoke, then. It was early in the morning, still dark outside, but my fever had broken and the pain from the cuts was gone. I got up to drink some water, then returned to bed, still weak. Before I drifted off again, I made my plan:

I'd call ó Cuinn in the new day.

October 30

Day

Conor was surprised to hear from me.

"We need to meet today," I told him.

We made arrangements to have lunch at a coffee shop near me. We'd meet there at two, it would be fairly empty by then. We'd need to talk where we wouldn't be heard, because we'd be discussing murder.

ó Cuinn was right on time. I knew the waitress—Ricky and I ate here frequently—and asked her for a back booth. The place was quiet, just us and a few other groups closer to the front. Conor ordered black coffee, I asked for an iced tea.

"You look tired," he said, once the waitress left with our drink orders.

"More than tired…I fought the *sidh* last night. They got in a few good jabs, but I won."

The way his jaw dropped would have been comical under other circumstances. "You…you banished them?"

I nodded. He forced his jaws closed. "How…?"

"I improvised. It worked. They clawed me in a few places, but Mongfind left a cure for that, and it worked, too."

"So…?" He left his question unasked, but I knew what it was.

"Yes," I told him, before adding, "so let's talk about the Samhain ritual."

The grin that crossed his face made him look uncomfortably like the *sidh*, and for a moment I regretted this meeting.

"Well, that's brilliant. You know it won't work without you."

"Do you have...everything?"

He was about to respond when the waitress brought our drinks. Conor stopped abruptly, averting his gaze, nervous and guilty, and I wondered how he'd possibly stayed out of jail if he'd acted this way with Bertolucci. Once she'd gone, he leaned close and whispered. "Yes, everything's been arranged."

"Everything," of course, included a human sacrificial victim. One I would be required to help kill.

I almost asked him how he'd manage that part—maybe he'd lure a junkie or transient with money; he was slightly built, and I couldn't picture him physically subduing anyone—but I really didn't want to hear details.

I know now, of course, that I was an idiot. I should have asked him. If I'd known what he had planned...

But I didn't, whether from cowardice or simply revulsion. I didn't ask him who we'd be killing.

"There is one thing only you can bring," he said.

"What?"

"Recall that the ritual indicates the use of a wand; it's crucial in creating the circle that will protect us. I can't supply you with that—you must find your wand on your own."

"Is that Mongfind or J.K. Rowling?"

He grimaced briefly, then added, "Children's fiction aside, magicians often speak of wands finding them, rather than vice versa. The wand is most likely found near a special tree, or forested area."

"Why do you know that? How long have you been studying this stuff?"

He actually reddened at that, revealing a secret passion. "I...it was just a purely academic study. Until..."

"Of course."

He reached into his jacket and removed a long bundle wrapped in a white handkerchief. "This is mine. I acquired it several years ago, from the area of Tara[18] in Ireland." He pulled the white linen away to reveal a surprisingly plain, sturdy foot-

[18] According to Celtic mythology, Tara was the ancient seat of kings.

long twig. The only unusual feature was a sort of groove that wound around the narrower half. "This is ash. The spiraling around it is the result of vines growing in the trees; finding something like this is quite rare."

"Have you used it, Conor?"

He looked away, abashed. "Only once..."

"When you summoned the *sidh*."

"Yes."

"Well, at least we know it works." I enjoyed mustering that sarcasm; I still didn't like Conor ó Cuinn, despite the fact that we would soon be partners. "So...have you thought about where...this...will happen tomorrow?"

He nodded. "Mongfind specifies that it must occur in a sacred oak grove. There isn't much sacred here in Southern California, but at least there are plenty of oaks."

Touche. I had to admire the way he'd just repaid my sarcasm. "Thousand Oaks[19], perhaps?"

"Actually...yes. I'll e-mail you directions."

We sat silently for a moment; when we weren't discussing the supernatural, we really had nothing in common. After a while, Conor said, "You understand that there is an element of danger to us in this."

I wasn't sure if he meant the ritual or kidnapping someone to be offered as a blood sacrifice. "Do you mean...?"

"Summoning Bal-sab. That's why the first part of the ritual calls for the creation of a protected space."

Of course I'd read Mongfind's description of encountering Bal-sab, but I realized only now that I'd still thought of it as fiction. A real encounter with a physical representation of Death...do any of us know ourselves well enough to perfectly anticipate how we'll react when confronted with something genuinely terrifying?

"Then we'll just have to be sure we create that space well, won't we?"

---

[19] Thousand Oaks is a suburb to the west of the San Fernando Valley, about forty minutes from Los Angeles.

That shut him up.

The rest of the meeting was devoted to lunch. We ate quickly and quietly. A last meal? Or the last meal of an old world?

As we finished, Conor asked, "Do you know where you'll look for your wand? Maybe you've got a special park you like, a garden...?"

"I do know, but it's...neither of those things."

He realized I had no interest in sharing a private plan with him, and he accepted that without further argument. "Well...tomorrow afternoon, then."

He left. I followed him out of the restaurant, climbed in my car, and headed toward the 5 freeway. Even though it was just past three p.m., traffic was heavy, and I headed south at barely ten miles an hour.

What will this all be like, if we succeed? Will there still be traffic jams, road rage, smog, hundred-degree fall temperatures thanks to global warming, gas at five dollars a gallon, increasing ranks of homeless, greedy corporate heads, ambitious politician, junkies, cancer, and all the other things that grind us down every day even as we take them for granted?

It was hard to imagine a renaissance in the middle of the SoCal metro sprawl.

October 30
-
October 31

I left the freeway at Cesar Chavez Avenue and headed east. My destination was only a mile from the freeway.

When Conor had mentioned a "special tree," my thoughts had immediately gone to a photo I'd taken sometime in the early 1980s. Back then, I'd briefly considered going into professional photography for my day job, and I'd worked to assemble a portfolio. One day, completely by accident, I'd stumbled across an amazing cemetery just east of downtown L.A. At the time I didn't know that Evergreen Cemetery was the oldest extant cemetery in Los Angeles, but its melancholy beauty, age, and hodgepodge of monuments and headstones had yielded some of my best photos.

My real prize, however, was a picture of a gigantic spreading oak that overlooked a significant chunk of the graveyard. In the final black-and-white print, the tree looked impossibly huge, and somehow wise.

I knew exactly where to find my wand.

At this time of the afternoon, on a weekday, the cemetery was mostly deserted. I was also saddened to see that it had fallen into some disrepair in the years since I'd last visited, but I spotted the oak easily enough, and parked as near to it as I could.

Evergreen dated back to 1877 and supposedly held some 300,000 interments. There were no superstars resting here, no shining beacons of Hollywood history, but Evergreen was home to many of L.A.'s more interesting historical figures. A tall, white monument marked the plot of the Lankershim family; Isaac

Lankershim had once had a town named after him, until that town was renamed North Hollywood in 1927.

I strode across the lawn, and was saddened to see patches of dying grass and headstones that had literally fallen in disrepair. A few graves were clean and well kept, testament to longstanding families that still honored their dead.

I passed the quaint, cobblestone cottage that would be opened for funerals, and elaborate granite memorials that were taller than I was. In some places, the headstones were so crowded together that it was hard to see ground beneath them. I passed a stone angel I'd shot thirty years ago, and saw it was now missing most of one upraised arm.

The oak had been significantly trimmed back, but it was still there, providing a surprisingly lush green canopy for those resting beneath. The sun was slanting in from the west now, but there were still areas beneath the oak hidden from light, perhaps permanently. The ground was spongy here, and I sidestepped around a large gray mushroom cropping up from the cracks in a plaque that marked an 1892 burial.

I didn't know what I was looking for, really, so I searched for a place to sit. There were no benches in this area, and I finally opted for a small patch of dry grass without a marker. Was it nonetheless a grave, one for which the marker had crumbled or been removed? I offered a silent apology to the resident beneath me, if that was the case.

I'd picked a spot in the sun, but the day's autumn warmth faded quickly, even as the sun's light did not. I shivered once, wondering why the temperature was dropping when sunset was still hours away.

The first tiny nudge—it wasn't truly a physical sensation, but I can only compare it to that—came then. I turned, expecting a visitor or a guard, but there was no one to be seen nearby, just a few distant joggers on the path that encircled the cemetery. A leaf, perhaps, that had fallen from the tree…

It happened again, this time feeling more like a small puff near my ear, like a sentient breeze trying to whisper its secrets.

Then I remembered something from Mongfind's book about contacting the dead:

"The new Druid will experience the initial attempts by the dead to reach us as the smallest of touches or sounds, or perhaps a movement half-glimpsed when nothing's there…those with experience, though, will understand that the dead are anxious to communicate, and that we need only open ourselves to them."

Open ourselves to them...I wasn't sure what that meant, and I wasn't sure I wanted to find out. Weren't close encounters with death at the heart of most great horror fiction? I'd certainly written about it myself dozens of times, everything from a story about a haunted bookstore[20] to flesh-eating zombies[21]. Again, I had to ask myself how much deeper I wanted to explore the real version of my fiction.

Yet I felt no fear about this potential meeting. Perhaps it was the gentleness of the approaches to me; there was something timid about it. Maybe the ghosts were more afraid of me.

And I hadn't come here to parlay with spirits; I was in search of a tool. But I had no idea how to go about finding what I needed; perhaps one already dead would know how to help me deal with a Lord of Death.

It was, paradoxically, too bright to see them, so I closed my eyes.

Whether what took place was dream or reality or trance or some other state, I can't say.

It was:

Gray, as if all light and color had been leeched from the world. And in this gray realm were gray people…hundreds, thousands, of them. They were dim—not translucent, not see-through shades with faint blue glows, not cheap movie effects, but rather like someone you'd glimpse from a distance standing in an unlit corner of an attic. I could see just enough of them to make out a few details: An out-of-fashion cut of hair, a nineteenth-century uniform, a woman's dress from the 1940s. Some of them

[20] "Blind-stamped", from *Shelf Life: Fantastic Stories Celebrating Bookstores*

[21] I confess I've written more zombie fiction than I care to list here.

moved slightly, wavering as if they were underwater. It was hard to tell how much awareness they possessed, but a few seemed to be murmuring. I could hear their voices, but too faintly to make out any words.

I watched them for a while before I rose to move among them. They didn't react…nor did I. There was nothing frightening about them; if anything, they seemed…sad. Stuck. How many of us feel like this in our lives: Drained, trapped, unaware? Death should be different, but perhaps it was just an extension of life.

As I walked through them, I saw a change happening, slowly: As the sky darkened, they brightened. Colors faded in on their clothing and skin; some took tentative steps.

And they began to notice me.

I wasn't sure when the first pair of faint eyes locked with mine, but I knew that they followed me as I walked by. More began to track me. A small, wizened woman in a shawl stretched out a veined arm as I passed.

I realized it was night now, and that was why they had changed, become slightly more substantial. I still felt no menace from them, but I did wonder how it was possible that night had settled in at the cemetery and I hadn't been asked to leave. Didn't they lock up graveyards at night? Wouldn't they have at least noticed my car, even if they'd somehow missed me?

I considered trying to find my car, seeing if I could leave, but I still didn't have what I'd come for. I'd walked out now from beneath the oak tree, and thought perhaps I should return to it.

Somehow I'd lost my bearings, and everything looked different in the gloom of night. Was that my tree ahead…or was it that silhouette against the sky behind me? The figures around me now were almost all Asian, some dressed in obsolete robes, and some in the loose-fitting clothing of nineteenth-century railroad workers. I also saw westerners here and there, but they didn't look like those I'd passed in other areas of Evergreen; these people were noticeably poor, with gaunt frames and threadbare garments of another age.

Potter's Field.

I remembered something I'd read about Evergreen: That it had once housed L.A. county's Potter's Field, where those too impoverished or just too forgotten to be buried elsewhere had been interred. But it wasn't just the transients and addicts and outlaws who rested there. Back in the nineteenth century, L.A.'s ruling whites had refused to integrate Chinese into their graveyards, and had charged the immigrants to be buried with the indigents. Now their spirits stood side by side, taking no notice of each other, proving that intolerance died with living skin.

A colder breeze caused me to tremble, but it wasn't just the temperature—that wind was tinged with something else, the mental equivalent of the smell of rotting meat. Then I saw the spirits being pushed aside by some greater mass. Something was flowing up out of the ground of the Potter's Field, something that was far blacker than the night sky. Even the dead were distressed now: I saw mouths open in soundless horror, hands upraised to ward off whatever it was that came.

What the fuck was I seeing? I ran down possibilities: An unidentified murderer or rapist who'd been interred in the Potter's Field, an accumulation of the misery the poor had suffered while alive, before the answer came: Surely this could only be Bal-sab. The black cloud was exactly what Mongfind had described, and a sense of immense hunger radiated from the heart of the thing. I turned to run, with no clear direction except away from it. My legs moved as if in a dream, they pumped furiously, my heart hammered, but my forward momentum was slow. Perhaps running through ghosts dragged on me, or Bal-sab had the power to pull me towards him.

I knew he would be on me in seconds; reason was replaced by the flight impulse. There was something mixed with Bal-sab's palpable hunger: he emanated glee at my panic, and I knew that if he caught me, he would toy with me, torture me, linger over every shriek and shiver, and it wouldn't end with my physical death. My suffering would make the pathetic souls of the Potter's Field seem blessed by comparison.

This was why the Druids had protected themselves before calling on him.

I could feel him closer behind me. My feet caught on headstones and tiny hills in the grass; I stumbled, but didn't go down. If I fell, it would be my final act.

Then, among the shades before me, I saw a woman who possessed more color than the rest. She faced me, fearless; she wore a sort of frock dress, and held something in one hand. I instinctively ran towards her, and she didn't falter as she turned her attention to my pursuer. She raised her hand, which I saw held a narrow rod, and she pointed it at the Death that came for me.

There was no sound or explosion of light, but the sensation of nightmarish pursuit vanished immediately. I knew without question that she'd somehow driven Bal-sab back, with only a gesture. I envied that confidence and power, regardless of the fact that she'd been dead for at least a century.

I walked towards her, full of questions, but when I opened my mouth I couldn't seem to speak. Who are you? How did you do that? Can you teach me? Are you a Druid?

She smiled as I approached, and held out her hand…no, not her hand, but the length of wood in it.

The wand.

At first I thought she meant to cast some sort of enchantment on me – a protection, perhaps – but then I realized her true intent: She wanted me to take the wand. I held up my own hand, looked at her tentatively, and she nodded. I reached out, wrapped my fingers around the slender length of wood—And woke up.

October 31

Morning

The sun was in my eyes, I was stiff and cold, and damp from morning dew.

I was still in the cemetery, where I'd apparently spent the night. That shouldn't have been possible…yet, as I sat up and looked around me at the headstones, the morning joggers, my great tree…it had happened.

The fingers of my right hand were tight. I flexed them, and something dropped from my grasp. I retrieved it.

It was the wand: A foot-long section of oak, twisted in a perfect spiral shape, with a neat nob at one end and a tapering point at the other. It was possible that it had fallen from the tree above me naturally-the wood felt slightly rough, and there was a slight center bend to it–but I recognized it without question:

It was the tool that my savior used during the night to drive Bal-sab back.

I didn't even ask myself if it had really happened or if I'd merely dreamed it. At this point, the answer didn't really matter.

I was relieved to find my car where I'd left it, and the gates to the cemetery were open. I drove out without seeing a caretaker or guard.

It was 7:33 as I left Evergreen, the morning of Halloween. The day was clear and already warm, with just a trace of L.A.'s perpetual smog blanket. I was surprised to find that I wasn't tired or aching from my night on the ground. In fact, I felt…well, I can only call it hyper-aware. I saw every detail as I drove towards the

5 freeway: Every yard of cracked asphalt, every scrap of trash, every used hypodermic needle or empty bottle, every man who staggered along the sidewalk too young to have dead eyes, every woman who carried a jar of Vaseline in a cheap purse and looked for her next trick, every kid whose heart hardened a little as he saw the bullies coming and wanted to join them.

At first I was glad to leave the city streets behind and ascend to the freeway that ran above the urban hell, but the morning rush-hour traffic was in full force and presented its own grim scenes: A woman on the shoulder, staring with grim desperation at her broken-down car; a man in a Lexus with a perfect haircut shrieking into a Bluetooth so loudly that I could hear him across two lanes of idling cars; honking horns, blaring ranchera music fighting discordant rock, a helicopter beating the air overhead.

This world was mad.

Two thousand years had led to this. It seemed ridiculous to think any of it could be reversed. The everyday difficulties of life, small and large, are too interconnected; severing one link can't destroy the chain. But if part of the chain can be weakened, then maybe we can begin the act of freeing ourselves. Isn't that why we vote, why we volunteer, why we donate?

What part of the chain would break if an ancient death god were appeased?

An hour later, I finally reached home. Roxie meowed unhappily at me, understandably upset over missing dinner last night, but even her irritated, shrill little cries lightened my mood. The world couldn't be so bad when different species could live together, with joys, upsets, and experiences shared, and those rare times when simply nothing happened except each other.

I fed Roxie, then she settled in at my feet, purring and grooming herself, as I checked e-mail. There was the message from Conor, with directions; he'd provided a map of the location where we were to meet. It was forty minutes or so to the west, but I'd be joining the going-home traffic and so doubled the time. I'd need to leave here at around 3:30, then.

I had six hours to prepare.

And no idea what "preparation" should be.

October 31

I spent part of the day apologizing. I'd missed two interviews, one last night and one this morning. I'd disappointed a New Jersey radio station and a Boston newspaper. And my publisher.

I called Ricky, but he only had a few minutes between takes. I lied, and told him everything was fine.

I studied the Samhain ritual in the journal. We'd begin with a prayer to the gods, we'd sanctify our space, we'd offer an animal in sacrifice, and then...I had no idea how Conor expected us to create the triple-death that the Celts had employed, the simultaneous strangling/stabbing/drowning, unless we were breaking into the backyard of someone who had both an oak grove and a swimming pool. Southern California isn't exactly known for its bogs and bodies of water.

Of course here I was considering participating in a murder, and I was more concerned with the method than the act.

I left early. I couldn't stay in the apartment anymore, thinking about what was to come. I took the wand and the netbook that had Mongfind's manuscript. Conor said he'd have everything else.

An hour later, I'd driven into the hills, down a road marked for construction, but which was still surrounded by undeveloped land. I parked, and hiked a short trail to the spot Conor had indicated. I had to admit that he'd chosen perfectly: The area was hidden in a slight depression, was surrounded on all sides by gorgeous old oak trees, and would be a lovely area to kill someone in.

I had to stop thinking that way.

Sacrifice has been practiced by cultures throughout history and around the world. Among the Celts, it had been considered a great honor to be chosen; those who were, accepted death willingly to ensure the prosperity of their clan.

This was the right thing to do.

But no matter how many times I repeated that to myself, it still felt like a lie.

I spent an hour there, trying to enjoy the sun, wondering if it would rise again tomorrow, watching a small brown lizard scuttle up the trunk of a tree, before ó Cuinn arrived. I heard an engine, and was surprised to see a rented four-wheel-drive SUV come bouncing up to the edge of the grove. Conor parked and got out.

"Ah, good—you're already here." He moved around to the rear of the SUV, opened it up, and revealed a cage holding a small goat. There was also a metal tub, a five-gallon bottle of water, and a duffel bag. Aside from the goat—a little gray-and-white kid who kept squalling piteously—he was alone, although I couldn't tell if there was someone else in the SUV.

"Aren't you…missing something?"

He nodded towards the front of the car. "I told our special guest to wait until I called for him. I thought that might be easier on you."

I started to walk toward the SUV to look in, but realized Conor was actually right about that. "Yes, it probably will be." The kid pressed its little face against the wire mesh of the cage and bleated at me. "A goat? Doesn't Mongfind mention sheep?"

Conor shrugged. "There aren't a lot of sheep in the L.A. area. The goat was hard enough to find. I don't think it much matters exactly what species the animal is."

"I hope you're right."

He set the tub in the middle of the grove, opened the five-gallon container, and poured the water into the tub. "Ahh," I said, watching him, "so that's how you plan to satisfy the drowning requirement."

"Yes. Again, when in L.A., like a good actor you learn to improvise. What about you—did you have any luck with the wand?"

I showed him my find, and his eyes narrowed as he examined it. "Where did you get it?"

"A cemetery, just east of downtown."

"You just found it there?"

"Well...not exactly...it was given to me in a dream, by a woman. I still had it when I woke up."

"A woman in a dream?"

I nodded. "Yes, but not Mongfind, or the Morrigan, if that's what you're thinking. From her dress, I'd guess this woman had lived about a hundred years ago, and I'm assuming she lived in L.A., since her grave is here."

Conor touched one finger lightly to the wand, held it there for a second, as if somehow gauging it, and then pulled his hand away. "She must have been a powerful wise woman. A witch, I guess you'd say."

I remembered how easily she'd repelled Bal-sab. "Yes, she was quite powerful."

"And now," he said, moving his eyes from the wand to my face, "so are you."

If he'd meant to flatter me with that, it didn't work. All he succeeded in doing was making me uncomfortable again; although I certainly had no objections to accruing power in some areas, magic I hadn't even believed in a week ago wasn't one of them. "Any power I have is...an accident."

"No. Not an accident. Call it what you like—destiny, fate, luck—but I believe that you were born for this night, just as I was. Most people go through life wondering if they have a real purpose; well, yours and mine is to set history back on its proper track. Tonight."

No, I wanted to say to him, I'm a writer. That's my purpose. Not this. But I wasn't interested in arguing with Conor ó Cuinn, so I kept quiet.

Overhead, the sky had started to dim, the blue taking on the deeper, almost metallic shade of approaching dusk in autumn.

The sun was dipping below the hill that defined the west side of the grove, and Conor turned his attention to the duffel bag. "We need to move quickly. It's almost time to begin."

He handed me what at first looked like a white sheet. "Put that on." I shook it out, and realized it was a simple robe, fashioned from bed linen, probably by Conor himself. I pulled it over my head, and he handed me a large sash I used to belt it. He'd even picked up three cheap lanterns that he now lit and set on the ground.

He put his own robe on, handed me a printed out version of the ritual, picked up his own copy…

We began.

Samhain

I won't give you the details here of the first part of what we did. It was hard not to giggle through some of it, although I thought of Bal-sab as we created the protective circle and any derisive laughter died in my throat. I'm not proud of my part in killing the goat. The poor little animal kicked and cried and shook, and even though its life ended quickly, it seemed like hours for me. Somehow assisting Conor with the sacrifice of the goat affected me far more than sharing a murder with the Morrigan had. I grew up with a hunter and tried to imagine this as no more than cleaning fish with dad, or watching him dress a deer; but I thought even my father would have a difficult time with a small, howling goat.

Conor, however, seemed to have no such compunctions. He performed his part of the ritual with clenched-jaw efficiency. I wondered if he'd done it before.

The goat's body, head submerged in the tub of water, had just ceased trembling when the air in the grove changed. The sky, still a faint shade of purple, abruptly darkened; the temperature dropped, my skin goose-pimpled.

Conor's steel melted. He looked up, eyes widening. "My God…" he breathed.

Yours, maybe. Not mine.

Bal-sab had arrived.

I went over the protection spell in my mind, hoping we'd done it right. The Lord of Death's unrelenting appetite would easily take us if we hadn't. We waited a few seconds, breathless—but the circle held. Bal-sab would be taking only what we offered.

"Let's finish this," I said to ó Cuinn.

His attention snapped back to me, and for a minute I saw him sag. After the way he'd dispatched the goat, I expected the next sacrifice to be easy for him. He didn't move, but only gazed towards the SUV.

"Conor…?"

Without a word, then, he trudged off to the parked SUV, opened the middle door, and reached in.

When I saw our intended victim, I understood his hesitation. My own resolution, which I'd spent the day—days—trying to build up vanished instantly.

"Your son…?"

Because it was a five-year-old boy he'd brought out of the SUV. The little boy—Alec, I remembered—looked like Conor, but like the Conor I'd seen in the photograph on his desk: Younger, fuller, happier. The boy still clutched some sort of little talking stuffed animal in one hand. He seemed small even for five.

Five.

"No," I said.

Conor clutched his son's hand in fingers still stained with goat's blood. At least his voice broke when he said, "We have to."

"No. This isn't what we talked about."

"It has to be an…extraordinary offering. We're trying to correct two thousand years of mistakes with one night."

I felt Bal-sab roil with anticipation above me. I felt the Morrigan's lingering presence within me, telling me Conor was right. This would work.

"Daddy?" said Alec, his accent thick even in two simple syllables. He looked up at his father with love and confusion.

I tore off the robe.

"What are you doing?" Conor released his son and started towards me.

"I'm leaving."

"You can't. I can't finish it alone. The ritual requires both of us."

I'd nearly reached the edge of the circle then. "I know. That's why I'm leaving."

"You won't be safe once you step out of that circle."

I knew that, too. And I'm ashamed to admit that I'm enough of a coward that I stopped. For a second. Long enough to say, "None of us are."

Then I stepped past the lines we'd drawn and walked out into the night.

I expected Bal-sab to engulf me. The last thing I'd feel would be agony, or intense cold, or the breath of eternal suffering.

Instead there was nothing. As soon as I was out from beneath the oaks, the sky returned to normal, I heard the distant sounds of freeways, saw the glow of the valley to the east…

And knew that I'd just damned the world.

Halloween

It's nearly midnight now on Halloween night. Two thousand years ago, the Samhain sacrifices would have been completed, and the feast celebrating summer's end begun. The Celts would have rested well knowing that they'd earned another year of prosperity and peace. The Lord of Death would visit them only for those whose long lives were at a natural end.

It won't be that way for us, though. Did I fail tonight? Could I really have granted the world a return to that kind of serenity?

At the beginning of this journal, I said this: "It's only been two weeks since the world started to fall apart." I realize now that sentence, while dramatic, is not entirely correct. The world fell apart long ago. And yet we continue to live in it; as messy and dangerous and ugly as it is, we somehow continue along, occasionally finding moments of joy, love, or just quiet reflection. We share love that bonds two of us together, and we share stories that one of us has created from nothing. We bond with non-human species, and we feel horror when we cause them harm.

I don't accept that I've condemned the world, because any world that requires giving the lives of children (or adults, or animals) to gods is frankly not worth living in. Gods are too arbitrary for me. Even the Morrigan's righteousness came with a vicious price.

I know Conor might try again, that he might find another woman who possesses skills greater than mine and the constitution to commit bloody sacrifice. If he succeeds, and the world improves overnight next year, or the year after that, then I will think of a young boy whose soul is owned forever by a black abomination, and I won't regret my decision.

I won't erase Mongfind's manuscript or break the wand I was gifted with, but I have no interest in casting spells or pursuing any other magical goals.

The world is already magical enough.

The End